Message to my readers.

Thank you to everyone who read and reviewed the first edition of *Caroline's Lighthouse*. The novel was a labor of love that took almost twenty years to come to reality from the moment of my idea until the moment I held the first printed copy in my hand in November of 2016, right after Thanksgiving.

I had both positive and negative feedback about the vivid descriptions my narrator, Caroline Douglas, offers in the first chapter. Caroline is a history buff who looks at the details of everything. I could rewrite the first chapter and remove or redistribute the descriptions, but I would rather just offer an updated layout, a new book size with a lower price point for the paperback, and a manuscript that has a fewer typos and editing issues since the first edition. Now, five years after the first publication, the novel is available in hardcover.

I have noted the constructive criticism for my next novels and plan to consider less bulky descriptions in the future. For now, I will let *Caroline's Lighthouse* speak for itself if my wonderful new readers who dislike vivid descriptions will just bear with me through the first chapter.

-Brandi Easterling Collins

Caroline's Lighthouse

by:

Brandi Easterling Collins

LUMINESCE
•PUBLISHING•

Luminesce Publishing books may be ordered
through booksellers or by contacting:

Luminesce Publishing
www.luminescepublishing.com

LUMINESCE
•PUBLISHING•

Back Cover image © Brandi Easterling Collins
Cover Illustrations Designed by renata.s & Freepik
Snowflake Illustration Designed by GarryKillian/Freepik
Cover and Interior design © Luminesce Publishing
Author photo © Felisha Weaver Photography

ISBN: 978-1-7322289-9-3 (hardcover)
ISBN: 978-1-7322289-2-4 (paperback)
ISBN: 978-1-7322289-3-1 (ebook)
Library of Congress Control Number: 2021933392

Acknowledgements

Thank you to my dear friends Alisha, Crystal, Felisha, Liz, Melissa and Sherry who have all contributed by reading drafts of this novel from its humble beginnings handwritten on notebook paper through the typed copies that have evolved throughout the last twenty years. Thank you to the Easterling, Russell, Campbell and Collins families for supporting my dream. Thank you to my mother, Opal, and mother-in-law, Joan, for believing in me. Thank you to my wonderful husband, Jonathan, who has supported me during the many late nights I spent writing and editing. Thank you to my beautiful children, Drew and Meredith, for being the inspiration to renew my passion for writing. Thank you to everyone who has supported me along the way.

Chapter 1

December 21, 1996

From the moment I laid eyes on Bettencourt Estate, I never wanted to leave. We opened a massive, spiked, cast-iron gate and drove through a dark tunnel of trees that lined both sides of the driveway. When Dad got out of the van to open the second gate, I stared in awe at what the headlights revealed. I had never in my life seen something so mysterious and scary, yet so breathtaking and beautiful.

Beyond the gate, the snow glistened with hints of pink, orange, and yellow from the sunset. The lighthouse stood in the distance, its once vibrant pattern of black and white diamonds barely visible in the impending darkness. Behind it, the ocean appeared to touch the sky at the horizon.

On the left, the silhouette of a single weeping willow tree, its top etched in snow, was small in comparison to the three-story house beside it. The house looked like a standard box colonial but with ornate trim and a front porch. I had never seen anything quite like it. As we inched closer, I noticed the white paint was peeling from the house in several places.

The stable was almost beside us, to the right of the house. The reddish-brown wooden building looked well-built, but the plain rectangular style did not match the house. According to my mother, the original stable had burnt to the ground long ago. There was so much to see; I couldn't take it in all at once.

As they looked around the estate, my older brothers, Jon and Brad, were awestruck as well. Looking at them, no one would have guessed they were twins. They would be eighteen in February. Jon took after our mother, with brown eyes and wavy blond hair he kept a bit long, just past his chin. Jon was tall like our father at almost six feet. Brad looked more like our father, with short, straight brown hair and hazel eyes. He was a few inches shorter and a bit stockier than Jon and Dad.

There was no mistaking that Jon and I were brother and sister because we looked so much alike. I had the same shade of brown eyes and wavy blond hair. I was petite like our mother at just over five feet tall. Keeping my hair long made me look even shorter, but I didn't care. I loved my hair main-ly because my mother had liked braiding it so much when I was younger. I missed having her around to do that. She had died in a car accident the summer after my twelfth birthday, three and a half years ago. I would be sixteen in May.

The estate had been in my mother's family for genera-tions. We were descendants of the original Bettencourt family who had founded the town and built the estate during the early 1800s. Mom's grandparents had left the property to her in their will. She had been their only grandchild and had spent summers with them when she was growing up.

Bettencourt was a small community located just outside of Norfolk, Virginia. It was similar in size to our hometown of Dardanelle, Arkansas. Both had populations of about four thousand people. Bettencourt had old buildings that had sur-vived the Civil War including the library, the courthouse, and the first town church that had been standing since the early 1800s like the estate. The town had a rich history, full of legends and ghost stories. It had taken us two days with an overnight stop at the halfway point to drive the twelve hundred miles from home.

I wondered how Mom might have felt, had she been able to visit Bettencourt again. My whole body ached as I thought of my mother. I had accepted her death and my father's remarriage, but sometimes the grief would resurface without warning and leave me with a sick feeling in the pit of my stomach.

As we got out of the van, my stepmother, Margo, mentioned how incredible the estate must have been when it was first built. Margo was tall and thin with sparkling aqua-blue eyes and dark brown curly hair she kept cut shoulder length. Her children, Jack and Trini, couldn't believe such a place existed. They both had their mother's dark hair and blue eyes, but Jack's hair was not curly. Trini's hair was so long—past her waist—it weighed down her curls. They were twelve and eight.

"I can see why your mother wanted you to see this place so badly," Margo said as she wrapped her arm around my shoulders. "It's marvelous, Caroline."

"It really is," I said.

We all had seen pictures of the estate, but it had been nowhere near the same as seeing it in person.

Dad and my brothers went into the house to make sure it was safe while the rest of us sorted through the luggage. One by one, the lights on the first floor shined through the front windows. Brad walked back to the van a few minutes later and told us it was safe to come inside.

A musty smell greeted us inside the old house. The dark hardwood floors were in remarkable shape considering their age, but the narrow planks were a bit uneven and seemed to have some bounce to them as we walked through the entryway into the parlor. A large floral area rug lay on the floor underneath a round table in the center of the room. A bright red potted poinsettia sat in the middle of the table.

The only things in the house that even resembled modern were still old to me. Metal tubes ran along the walls connecting the outlets and light fixtures. We found a stereo and television from the 1970s in the living room under dusty white sheets. We were amazed to learn the electronics still worked, although we couldn't pick up any stations.

In line with the door, on the right wall, was a staircase that looked like something out of a horror movie. The dark woodwork on the banisters resembled tiny stacked vases. The shadows were especially creepy when Jon and Dad came down the stairs carrying flashlights. A few light bulbs had blown when Dad had flipped the switch at the base of the stairs.

"The rest of the house seems fine, minus a few bulbs," Dad said. "This place looks exactly how I remember it."

My parents had not been to the estate since Mom's grandmother had died when my brothers were babies. I had asked Dad once why we never visited Bettencourt. He had told me life just got in the way. I was born when my brothers were two years old, and after that, it had been too hard for them to travel with three small children. Later, relatives had been in poor health. Dad had lost several elderly aunts and uncles when I was a small child.

Of my grandparents, Dad's father had died first, then Mom's father and mother. Dad's mother, Meema Douglas, was still living and in relatively good health, although she appeared quite frail. I remember she had held one of my hands during Mom's graveside service. Her hands had felt fragile with her skin stretched tightly over her large arthritic knuckles. Someone else had stood behind me that day and held my other hand with their soft fingers intertwined diagonally with mine. They had been a great comfort to me at the time. I wished I could remember who, so I could thank them.

After we had brought in our essential bags, we divvied out room assignments.

"You can have Mom's old room if you want it, Caroline," Jon said. "Top of the stairs to the right."

"Yes," I said. "I definitely want it."

I grasped the handrail tightly as I ascended the stairs, which loudly creaked. Several framed photographs lined the wall. There were a few family portraits of my mother as a child with my grandparents, some of her alone as a teenager, a wedding portrait of my parents, and one of my brothers when they were newborns. I felt lost in another time as I looked at them.

When I reached the dark hallway, I found the room. As soon as I touched the doorknob, my skin tingled, and all the hairs on my arm stood up. I eased the door open and peered inside. I couldn't find a light switch on the wall, so I turned on the flashlight Jon had given me. I saw dark pink walls and beautiful hardwood floors. Hanging on the wall in front of me was a colorful framed poster that read: Roberta.

I removed the sheets covering the furniture. It was mahogany-colored wood with carved details that looked like pineapple skin. All of it seemed as old as the house itself. A large timeworn trunk with a dark metal lock and bands sat on the floor at the foot of the four-post bed, which was centered on the right wall. On the left was a grand fireplace with intricate woodwork on the mantel that matched the furniture. The closet was on the same wall, closer to me. There was a built-in bookcase to the right of the fireplace, a small writing desk near the windows in front of me, and a dresser with a small mirror on the same wall as the door. I noticed there were oil lanterns mounted on the walls. The last thing that caught my attention was the large burgundy area rug that covered the floor between the bed and dresser.

As I sat on the bed, Jon came in carrying firewood. "I thought you might like a fire," he said.

"Yeah, it's freezing in here."

"Well, the gas heat is only on the first floor," Jon said. "But it does feel a lot colder in here than the other rooms."

"Really?" I asked. I figured the entire second floor would be cold due to the heating situation.

"Well, it is a room with a lot of windows," Jon said as he tapped lightly on one of them. "Single pane."

"Where are you sleeping?"

"Right next door. Brad too. It's the only room with two beds. Everyone else is at the other end. Brad wanted to stay close to protect you from the ghosts."

I loved my brothers equally, but I'd always felt closer to Jon since he and I had more in common. We were both quiet, reflective, and shy at times and liked the same older music— the stuff our parents had grown up with. Brad was louder and more outgoing. Of the three of us, he was the most popular. Both of them played baseball. Jon was better at it, but Brad seemed to enjoy it more. I think Jon had only started playing so he could hang out with Brad. Jon had never intended to be the star pitcher in their senior year of high school, but it was how things had worked out. They were great friends to each other but didn't have much else in common, except for their constant need to protect me and their strong bond from having shared the womb, which I would never understand.

As Jon worked on my fire, I looked around the room and realized there were no outlets, no phone jacks, and no modern lights. There was no electricity whatsoever. I was confused because Mom had never mentioned not having electricity in her room.

"There's no electricity in here," I said.

Jon looked around at the walls. "Maybe the closet's wired," he said as he opened the closet door.

He was right. There was a single light bulb hanging from the ceiling and one outlet on the wall in the tiny closet. There was something else strange about the room. My skin felt clammy, and I felt tightness in my chest, but I couldn't quite determine what was making me feel that way. I took a few deep breaths to calm down.

"This is so weird," I said.

"What's going on?" Dad asked from the hallway.

"Dad," I said. "This room isn't wired for electricity like all the other rooms. The closet has power, but that's the only place."

"Nope, it never was," Dad said. "Your mother used to run an extension cord from the closet for a bedside lamp and to plug in her record player. Do you want to move to the library sofa, or go to the living room?"

"I'll stay here. If Mom managed, I can too," I said.

"Now that's the spirit!" Dad said. He left the room and then called back to us. "Bob and his family are on their way with food, so come downstairs soon!"

Chapter 2

Dad's friend, Bob Russell, had been working on the house for the past few weeks. He and his family lived in Bettencourt and had kept watch over the place for us. Bob had recently overseen plumbing and wiring updates. He had also ensured the propane heating system for downstairs functioned safely. The roof Mom's grandparents had replaced showed signs of damage, so Dad had taken out a small mortgage on the estate to pay for a new roof and some other much-needed repairs. Dad wanted to turn the place into a bed and breakfast and rent it out through a property management firm to help earn extra money to save for retirement and help us kids with college.

Bob and his wife, Marlene, had gone to college with my parents. They had become friends with my mother when she had stayed with her grandparents every summer from the time she was six years old. When Mom had moved to Bettencourt to live with her grandparents while she attended college, Dad had come with her because they were so in love they didn't want to be apart for four years. They had gotten married at Bettencourt Estate after they graduated and had moved back to Dardanelle not long afterward for Dad's job offer.

We had last seen the Russell family at Dad and Margo's wedding almost a year and a half ago. Marlene was a short, plump woman with rosy cheeks and dark eyes. She kept her dark hair big and wore bright red tortoise shell glasses from the 1980s that hid how pretty she was. Bob was tall and stout with greying blond hair and blue eyes.

They reminded me of an old sitcom family. Marlene ran their household, baked, sewed, and used her accounting degree to handle the billing and office work for Bob's construction company, which was the largest and most respected in town. She was the type of person who everyone instantly liked when they met her. Bob worked all the time and liked to joke around with anyone younger than him, and offered a very fake chuckle when someone told a joke he didn't understand. He loved his wife and told everyone he met that he married the most beautiful woman he had ever seen.

I had first met them during a visit for their summer vacation when I was eight. They had come again when I was ten. The other years we had met them somewhere within a day's driving distance from our home to vacation together. Back then, I had thought of Marlene and Bob like an aunt and uncle. Their son, Robert Russell III, known to everyone as Bo, was about ten months older than me. He became one of my best friends. I always felt like I had known Bo forever. Even though we only saw each other once every year or so, we were always able to pick up where we left off with our friendship. I had a lot of fun during those vacations with my brothers and Bo. We had been planning a trip to see them the summer my mother had died.

Bo had been such a good friend during the weeks after Mom's death. His family had flown out and stayed for almost two weeks. Bo and my other best friend, Becca, had been the only friends who hadn't tried to cheer me up. Bo had just sat beside me and let me lean on his shoulder and cry while he stroked my hair. I couldn't imagine any other thirteen-year-old boy being that sensitive. He never said anything about my mother's death after the initial "I am so sorry" when he first hugged me. After he had gone home, we began talking on the phone at least once a week.

I had known Becca since kindergarten when she'd insisted that we become friends. Her dark auburn hair seemed to shine redder in the sunlight. Becca's outgoing personality had been a good contrast to my painfully shy one growing up. She had trouble being around me after my mom died because seeing me cry made her cry too. I could always tell when Becca had been crying because her green eyes seemed more vibrant afterward.

After Dad and Margo's wedding, Becca told me she thought Bo liked me as more than a friend, which I thought was crazy. She insisted that Bo and I talked on the phone way too much to be just friends, but the distance between our homes was the reason for all the phone calls. Bo and I couldn't talk at school every day like I could with Becca. She told me I needed to open my eyes because Bo was a very attractive guy. I hadn't really thought about his attractiveness. He was the sweetest guy I knew but was just a friend. I had always loved him like I loved my brothers. Anything more than that seemed weird to me. He was just Bo.

I hardly recognized Bo when he walked into the house. My heart began pounding as soon as I saw him, which surprised me. I had no idea how much he had grown up and changed. When I had last seen him at my dad's wedding, Bo was still skinny and awkward with short blond hair on a head that had looked too big for his body. He had worn unflattering glasses and braces to straighten his teeth. But I had been skinny and awkward then, too, with braces of my own. Now, Bo stood almost as tall as his father. The braces were gone and his blue eyes shined behind silver wire-rimmed glasses that complimented his face. His dark blond hair was a bit longer, and he was more muscular than before. Bo looked like a model who had just stepped out of a clothing catalog.

"It's so good to see you, Caroline," Bo said as he rushed over to greet me first. "I've missed you."

I felt lightheaded when he hugged me and lifted me off the ground a bit. I certainly didn't think of him as family at that moment. I wanted to reach up and run my fingers through his hair. He was so cute, and his voice sounded so much deeper than it had on the phone just a few days ago. Bo smelled so good that I didn't want to stop hugging him. I had missed him too.

Jack elbowed me. "You're drooling," he whispered.

Jack was right; I had temporarily lost control of the muscles around my mouth.

"Shut up!" I mouthed to him and tried to hide the fact that I was blushing.

Trini snickered but quickly stopped when I glared at her.

As soon as everyone had finished greeting each other, Bob began joking around. "So," he said. "Are you guys ready for your vacation in an old haunted house?"

"Bob!" Marlene scolded. "Hush now, you'll frighten the children."

"Well, I guess we're ready," Dad said. As a science teacher, he thought there should be a rational explanation for everything, so he never believed any of the ghost stories. "You still coming over tomorrow to discuss final plans for the renovation? Maybe we can scare the ghosts away so they won't scare our guests."

Bob laughed. "I guess I can make time for you," he said. "Around here, though, you might get more guests if you market the place with the ghosts included."

The adults and Trini ate in the dining room, while Bo joined the rest of us in the living room. We removed the sheets from the furniture and found places to sit around the coffee table. The living room contained two brown leather sofas, an oversized armchair, and two beautiful striped upholstered chairs near the fireplace.

Bo had been working on the house with his dad and was anxious to tell us about it. "This place is in really great shape considering how old it is," he said. "The kitchen was updated in the late 60s or early 70s, so at least it works even if it's not pretty."

"Kind of like the furniture," Jack said.

"True," Bo said.

Bo was right about the kitchen. I thought it was hideous. It had appliances the grossest shade of avocado green I had ever seen and dark cabinets with burnt-orange laminate countertops. The floors were geometric-patterned linoleum in the same color scheme. It was decorated like a fast-food restaurant, almost painful to my eyes.

I couldn't stop watching Bo as he passionately described the original woodwork on the staircase spindles. I'd had a crush on a boy at school once, but it had passed when I realized what a jerk the boy was, and I hadn't told anyone about it. It had been different than what I felt for Bo. It was strange being so attracted to him, considering how long he had been my friend.

"What places should we check out while we're here?" Jon asked.

"You need to see our church and cemetery," Bo said. "It's the oldest one in town."

"You want us to visit a graveyard?" Brad asked, his eyes wide with concern. "Why?"

"It's awesome. There're all these old, old graves to look at. Some of them are so old the names have worn off. A lot of the graves don't even have headstones," Bo said. "Me and my friends go there every Halloween."

"Y'all don't screw around with anything there do you?" Jon asked.

Jon had never been in any trouble. In fact, I couldn't imagine him ever breaking a rule.

"No, man, we don't mess around with the dead," Bo said. "I know you've heard the stories about this place from your mom. There are a lot of hauntings around the rest of the town too. We mainly go there to protect our church and keep anyone else from vandalizing anything. It's the same cemetery where the Bettencourts are buried."

We nodded. Jack tried to act cool, but he looked a bit scared after Bo mentioned the other hauntings. Dad and Jon had never cared much for ghost stories, but Mom had told us plenty. Brad and I had always liked hearing the stories, especially about Caroline Marshall, our relative who had died tragically.

According to Mom's stories, Caroline Marshall was the youngest granddaughter of the Bettencourts. Her parents, Colin and Josette Marshall, had already arranged the marriage of their oldest daughter, Bonnie, to a doctor. They had forced Caroline to accept the marriage proposal of an attorney from a neighboring town. But Caroline was in love with Thomas Cooper, the caretaker of the lighthouse and an orphan whom the family had taken in several years prior.

The Marshalls fired Thomas and refused to allow Caroline to marry him. The day after Christmas in 1846, the Marshalls and their new lighthouse caretaker were stranded away from home because of a snowstorm. Bonnie gave birth to twins that same evening, a boy and a girl. No one knew for sure exactly what happened that night because the servants were busy attending to Bonnie, but they found Caroline dead the next morning. It appeared she had committed suicide by jumping from the top of the lighthouse. She was only seventeen.

When Thomas returned to Bettencourt a few days later, it was presumed he had planned to take Caroline away with him. Instead, he learned of her death and was so distraught he killed himself the same way. After that, the lighthouse was locked and never used again. Every year since then, though, people in town had reported seeing light coming from the lighthouse the night after Christmas and early into the next morning.

Police investigations had never turned up any trespassers. Mom had never been at the estate right after Christmas to see anything, but her grandparents and several other people in town, including the Russells, said it happened every year like clockwork. My grandmother, who had grown up in the house, wouldn't talk about it at all.

The whole estate was riddled with tragedy, which added to the rumors of it being haunted. Caroline's parents and a young girl they adopted died in the fire that destroyed the stable some time later, and then a lot of the remaining family died in a disease outbreak in the early 1900s. Mom's grandmother was the only remaining survivor at the time according to my mother's research. She had traced our family history back to Bonnie's daughter, Antoinette. Bonnie's son, Weston, had died as a teenager during the Civil War.

Mom had named me after Caroline Marshall, which got creepier the more I thought about it.

I had been lost in my thoughts. I glanced back at Bo. *God, he's so cute,* I thought.

"Plus," Bo said. "You don't destroy things in this town and get away with it. The cops around here know everything that goes on. Sometimes they know things before they even happen. Besides, you know I wouldn't hang around with losers who would do crap like that."

"So who are you hanging around with?" Brad asked. "Anyone special?"

Bo looked at me and then turned to Brad. "Nah," he said. "Just friends and my cousin. You still with Kate?"

"Yeah," Brad said.

Brad and Kate had been together for two years. Our whole family loved her. I especially enjoyed how she could kick Brad's butt at one-on-one on the basketball court. She was a perfect match for him. She was smart and athletic, with long dark hair and pale green eyes. It was interesting how they had met. Jon had gone out with Kate first as part of a group date, but they realized they were better as friends when Brad had met up with them and instantly formed a connection with Kate. Jon had just shrugged off the whole thing because he was more interested in preparing for college than dating anyone seriously.

"That's great," Bo said. "She seemed nice when I met her at the wedding."

"She is," Brad said.

It was nice to see Bo and his parents again, even if I barely spoke with them. Bo hugged me again before they left. Him hugging me was nothing new; he had always done that, but now it felt different. After they had left, all I wanted was a nice warm bath before bed.

The bathroom was old but immaculate. I immediately knew Marlene had cleaned it and the kitchen before our arrival. I loved the old chrome fixtures, the claw-foot bathtub, and the pedestal sink. The small shower was separate, with white tiled walls and matching fixtures. Lining the walls, chest height on me were the same rectangle-shaped tiles from the shower walls. Above the tiles, the walls were painted mint green. The floors were hexagon-shaped black and white tiles in a pattern that made me feel dizzy. I could tell a few updates had been made throughout the years, but for the most part, I imagined the bathroom looked like it had when it was first added to the house during the 1920s.

As soon as the tub was full of steaming hot water, I turned off the lights and lit a couple of the vanilla-scented candles that were sitting around the room. The candlelight and the light from the gas heater on the wall gave the room a nice warm glow. I needed the bath after the long day of traveling. As I relaxed in the tub, I recalled one of the stories Mom had told me about the house involving missing pies.

Mom's grandpa had often been accused of stealing pies left to cool on the kitchen windowsill, but he had sworn his innocence, even when the empty pie pans were found hidden in the stable where he had his workshop. He had always claimed a ghost must have taken the pies. It had happened all the time during the holidays.

By the time I got back to my room, it was warm from the fire. Someone had put more wood in the fireplace for me. I couldn't wait until morning because I wanted to explore the house so badly. How could I possibly go to sleep when there was an old closet full of things just waiting to be opened? Something about the history of the whole place fascinated me. I hoped to solve some of the mysteries as we packed away all the things that had been left behind. More than anything, I hoped to learn more about my mother and the house she had loved so much.

I put clean sheets on the bed and laid out all of my clothes that needed to be hung up. I always felt more at ease when my things were put away. The tiny closet held a few pieces of clothing only old enough to have belonged to my mother. I laughed when I realized some people at my school wore the same style of clothing that Mom had worn when she was a teenager.

I found a cardboard box at the bottom of the closet. It was so heavy I could only manage to drag it to the area in front of the fireplace. I knew I would have to leave it there because I wanted to look through it by myself before I told anyone else about it. I was excited to open the box, mainly because I hoped to find more things that had belonged to my mother.

I was delighted to find in the box photos of Mom as a teenager. She had been alone in at least half of the photos, and with friends or family in the other half. I recognized Bob and Marlene in some that had been taken at an old cemetery. I glanced at each photo and laid it aside carefully. When I reached the bottom of the box, I found the most important thing, a small black leather book with the initials R.M.B. stamped on the cover.

"Roberta Mavis Baker," I whispered to myself. "This was Mom's diary."

For reasons I couldn't begin to explain or understand, I couldn't open the diary. I didn't feel ready to read it. I put the photos back in the box and slid it back into the closet where I had found it. I crawled into bed with my mother's diary clutched against my chest. At first, I had trouble going to sleep. My mind was racing with plans for the rest of our vacation. I could tell already; it would be like none other.

Chapter 3

December 22, 1996

I woke suddenly from a deep sleep. The room was bright from the sunlight that shined through the windows. It felt like someone had just grabbed my ankle with their ice-cold hand. I sat up in bed and pushed the blankets back on my feet, but still felt the coldness through my socks. It took me a moment to catch my breath and calm down as I looked around the room. There was no one in the room with me. The fire had gone out during the night.

I must have been dreaming, I thought. I didn't want to consider any other explanation.

With my robe and a blanket wrapped tightly around me, I walked to the window and looked at the incredible view. I could see the lighthouse and the ocean in the distance. A tiny house sat near the water. I assumed it was the boathouse Mom had mentioned. Her grandparents had stopped using it out of frustration because the doors seemed to have locked on their own all the time.

Seeing the serene view made me understand why Mom had chosen the room. The whole scene looked like an artist's painting with the snow-covered ground and whitecaps on the water. The room was not as frightening in the morning light, but I still sensed something was off and whatever it was made me feel extremely uneasy.

The last time I remembered feeling that way had been in the seconds after the doorbell rang on the day my mother had died. Mom had called and told us she would be late, but we had begun to worry when she wasn't home three hours later and none of her friends we called had seen her. I had stood behind Dad as he let two police officers into our house that evening. I didn't remember exactly what the officers had looked like; I just remembered the underlying sadness in their eyes.

"Mr. Douglas," the male officer had said. He had begun to speak again but stopped after seeing me in the entryway. His green eyes had conveyed compassion.

"May we speak privately?" the female officer had asked. Her friendly eyes had been such a light brown they appeared almost orange.

Dad had led them to our living room. The way the officers had looked at me as they passed had told me more than any words could have. I had thought notifying families of deaths must have been the most terrible part of their job. I couldn't remember what else they had said; I just remembered praying it had been a nightmare I could wake from. All I had heard afterward was my pulse pounding in my head. I had felt sick and dizzy as I'd watched my father bury his face in his hands and sob. My brothers had been standing behind me, one on each side. If they hadn't each had one hand on my shoulders, I could not have remained on my feet.

The days after that had been so difficult. Brad and I had shown our emotions more freely than Jon. I'd seen Brad cry several times, but I had never seen Jon cry, not even when we were little kids. At Mom's funeral, while Brad and I had cried, Jon had stood stoically beside Dad—who had looked like he'd aged ten years in three days. I only had a few memories from that time because it had been so painful.

21

I was startled when someone knocked on the bedroom door.

"Caroline," Jon said. "Are you awake?"

"Yes, come in."

"Good morning," Jon said. He was wearing boots and thick pants. His hair was wet from the melting snow and stuck to the side of his face.

"Been exploring?" I asked.

"Not unless you call shoveling snow off the walkway exploring. It snowed a little more last night," he said as he pushed his hair behind his ears. "Brad tried to wake you up earlier, but said you were dead to the world."

So Brad had grabbed my ankle. I was relieved.

"The Russells are on their way. I thought you'd want to get dressed before Bo gets here," Jon said with a smirk.

"Whatever," I said. I felt myself blushing. "He's just my friend and like another big brother to me, thank you. It would be like incest or something."

Jon laughed. "Your face says it all," he said. "Bo couldn't stop looking at you last night. Even Brad noticed, and he's usually pretty oblivious to that kind of stuff. I know they've always been Uncle Bob and Aunt Marlene to us, but we're not actually related. Bo likes you, and you obviously like him too."

"He probably has a girlfriend," I said with a sigh.

There had to be girls who liked him based on his looks alone, and if those same girls knew him as I did, I was certain it was true. But he had never mentioned a girlfriend when we had spoken on the phone. We had talked about everything but that.

"He doesn't," Jon said. "Didn't you hear what he said to Brad about not hanging around with anyone special? You talk to him on the phone all the time, wouldn't you know? I thought it was weird, but when he and I were alone in the kitchen, he asked if you were seeing anyone. He wants us to go to a bonfire thing with his friends on Monday and wants me to meet his cousin."

I had heard what Bo had said about who he hung out with, but I was still having trouble sorting out how I felt about him. Honestly, I had never thought of Bo as a potential boyfriend before. The thought of seeing him again soon made me nervous.

"He just threw in that question about you with the other stuff," Jon said. "He seemed relieved when I told him you weren't dating anyone."

"Yeah, and things would work out so well between us since he lives so far away."

"You never know. Kate's going to college next year and Brad's still thinking about the Navy. They're going to try to make it work."

"Maybe we should try to find you a girlfriend instead of trying to find me a boyfriend."

Jon laughed. "I've had enough girl talk for the day," he said. "You want to paint each other's nails next?"

I rolled my eyes. "Oh, Jon, you wouldn't believe what I found in the closet last night. Did you know Mom used to keep a diary?" I asked.

"No, she never mentioned it to me," he said. "But I wouldn't think she would've told me. Did you read it?"

"I didn't read it, but I did look at a bunch of old photos of Mom and her friends," I said. "A few of them were taken in the cemetery. Probably the one Bo wants us to see."

"We'll have to look at them later," Jon said as he walked out the door. "Wear something warm. We get to fix the shutters on the back of the house."

"Do I have to?" I asked as I plopped back down on the bed. "I really wanted to look around inside."

"Well, I have to since the banging shutters were scaring Trini last night," he said. "And you're the only person who can help me unless you can think of some way to trick Brad into climbing a ladder or leaning out of a window."

"You've got a point there," I said.

Brad was terrified of heights. He had fallen out of a tree house and broken his arm when he was younger.

Everyone had arrived by the time I went downstairs. Dad and Bob were sitting at the dining room table discussing the renovation. Margo and Marlene were in the kitchen getting breakfast together. I heard Bo talking with my brothers and the kids in the living room.

"Good morning, Caroline," Bob said. "Mark was telling me you noticed your room never had electricity, except for the outlet in the closet."

"Yes," I said. "Mom never mentioned it."

"Do you want us to wire your room today?" Dad asked. "Bob says there's enough room in the fuse box if you want us to."

"No," I said quickly. "Don't."

"You're sure?" Bob asked. "We could have it finished before the electrician comes to inspect the work this afternoon. Throw in a couple more outlets so that you could have a lamp by the bed? We need to do it eventually anyway to maximize the rental."

"I don't want you to right now," I said as I sat down with them at the table. "Can we just wait? I mean nothing's been done on the third floor yet anyway, right?"

"Suit yourself," Dad said and then turned to Bob. "What else do we need to go through while we're here? What about the heat and air?"

"The window units Roberta's grandparents used during the summers are pretty much shot, and they're a big eyesore. You'll need two units to cover the upstairs and main floor, a third unit if you want to heat and cool the third floor. The existing propane heating system is still okay for now on the main floor if you want to continue using it to save some money. You have to keep the propane for the cooktop and the water heater anyway. I added some carbon monoxide detectors for your peace of mind."

"We've been talking about all that. I think right now, we leave the third floor alone for storage and not worry about heating it since there's no plumbing up there to worry about. I think it used to be servant space. Later on, we can renovate it and open it up for rental. All the costs are adding up. We still need to add another bathroom or two. And at least another fifteen or twenty grand for the heat and air, right, even if we keep the propane heat for the main floor?"

"At least," Bob said as he jotted down notes on his notepad. "You have to make a decision about the boathouse too."

It was interesting listening to Bob and Dad talk about all the decisions for the house. I sat there and looked back and forth at them as they spoke.

"I still don't know about using it. The liability involved with opening the boathouse," Dad said. "Is it worth it or should we tear it and the dock down?"

"The dock is structurally sound. It's only about thirty years old or so," Bob said. "I remember watching it get re-built when I was a kid. If you get the grant that Marlene found through the historical society to restore the lighthouse, you'll have to keep the boathouse. I think it was built around the same time. The boathouse wouldn't be much good without a dock."

"I didn't think about that," Dad said. "I know we want to keep the lighthouse. Roberta loved it. I just hope the engineer's inspection of it is promising. The outside just looks like it needs fresh paint. What are your thoughts on the inside?"

"About that," Bob said. "We haven't been inside. The lock is even more corroded than it was when we were kids. I didn't want to break it by trying to pick it without talking to you first. We may have a chance if we can find the key and spray some lubricant inside it to clean out the gunk, but most likely, we'll need to break the lock."

"Let's wait on that for now," Dad said. "The engineer is coming a week from Monday, right?"

Bob nodded and took a drink of his coffee.

My heart sank. I wanted to go inside the lighthouse so badly it didn't matter about all the rumors of the haunting. Entering a place that had not been opened for a hundred and fifty years was so compelling I was almost willing to break down the door myself.

Chapter 4

After breakfast, Bo and Brad shoveled snow away from the house while Jon and I repaired the shutters. Jon stood on the ladder, and I held the shutters through the window from inside the house. The room Trini had slept in was narrow and much smaller than the other rooms. As we worked, I noticed dark circles under my brother's eyes.

"Jon, are you okay?" I asked.

"I'm fine," he said. He slipped with the drill and then pounded the shutter with his fist. "Damn it!"

"You look really tired," I said. "Did you not sleep well?"

"Brad's snoring kept me up half the night."

He was lying to me, but I let it go. We worked together without speaking and quickly finished the repairs.

As we packed up the tools, we were pelted with snowballs from below. Jack had started a fight with Bo and Brad, and then Trini had gotten involved in the action. Trini had tried to run away, but couldn't outrun Brad. Jack had forgotten how good my brothers were at baseball and soon surrendered and begged for a truce. I watched as Bo shielded Trini to get her to safety and thought he was sweet. I was glad to be able to close the window and get out of the cold.

Later, as we stood by the fire in the living room, I noticed that Brad looked as tired as Jon had earlier.

"Looks like you didn't sleep well," I said.

"Yeah," he said. "Jon was snoring."

"Funny," I said. I was certain Brad was lying.

"Not really," Brad said.

"No," I said as I crossed my arms. "Funny you both told me the same lie."

Brad sighed. "Look, we both had some bad dreams," he said. "No big deal. Crappy beds and all that traveling messed with our heads."

"If it's no big deal, why lie?" I asked. "Cut the crap, Brad."

"Fine," he said. "I don't know what Jon dreamed about, but I was at the top of the lighthouse holding your hands. You had fallen over the side. I was trying to pull you up, but you fell. Then I woke up."

"Well that's morbid," Bo said as he joined us in the living room. He put his arm around my shoulders, which caught my hair. "I hope you're not planning to follow in the footsteps of Caroline Marshall."

I couldn't answer him. He had his arm around me. He had done the same thing for a picture at the wedding, but now my skin tingled every time he touched me.

"It was just a stupid dream," Brad said. He looked embarrassed. "I was just thinking about those stories Mom used to tell us."

"Well, I'll do my best not to fall over the side of the lighthouse," I said.

"You better not because there's no way in hell I'm climbing that thing," Brad said.

Dad walked in. "No one is climbing anything," he said. "Not until the engineer confirms it's safe." He raised his eyebrows and stared at Bo.

Bo removed his arm from my shoulders and took a couple of steps sideways until he was no longer standing so close to me. Dad seemed satisfied with that. He roughly patted Bo on the back and then left the room.

Dad had always been great at interrupting conversations at opportune moments. He had overheard my brothers and me discussing his and Margo's relationship right after he had brought her and the kids over to meet us for the first time. They had met in a grief counseling group about six months after Mom had died. The therapist we saw at the time had warned us to prepare for the fact that our father might start dating again.

Dad had yelled at us that night. "You can hate Margo, hate Jack and Trini, and most of all hate me! You can cry and scream and throw things, but nothing, nothing will bring your mother back! Believe me, I would cut off both arms and legs if it would bring her back to us, but it won't! Your mother—the only woman I've ever loved—is gone!"

"We know that better than anyone, Dad," I had said. "It's you who's forgotten. It hasn't even been a year!"

"The time doesn't matter," he had said. "I don't have to explain myself to you. I'm the parent here. It's not like I'm bringing home a mass murderer. Margo might as well be a saint. She's a kindergarten teacher! She's been raising those kids by herself since her husband died, always putting them first just like I have with you. Just give her a chance, and you might like her."

"Whatever," Brad had said.

"All of you get out of my sight," Dad had said. His eyes had appeared glassy like he could have cried at any moment. "Go to your rooms!"

I had cried on the phone to Becca that night. She had told me she loved me but said I was being a brat and should apologize to my dad. I had called Bo next, and he had said he understood why I was upset but ultimately agreed with Becca. I had been upset with both of them, but they were right.

Later that evening, I went to my father's room and found him sitting in his armchair with an open book in his lap. I didn't think he had been reading. I felt pretty ashamed of myself for the way I had behaved earlier. I couldn't remember the last time I had sat on my father's lap before that night, but at that moment I felt like a little girl again in need of forgiveness. I started crying before I reached his outstretched arms.

"Baby, this isn't the way I thought your life would be. It isn't the way I planned my life to be either. I wanted you and your brothers to have childhoods without all this heartache."

"I know." I hugged him tighter.

"I sometimes wish it had been me who died instead of her, then you kids would be better off."

"Daddy, don't say that. I'm so sorry."

"Your mother would know exactly what to say. I just don't know. I feel happy when I'm with Margo. That's not something I thought I could ever have again and I think she feels the same way."

He hugged me tightly, whispered he loved me and said that everything would be okay. By that point, Jon and Brad had come to the doorway to apologize too. By the end of our conversation, we had agreed to give Margo a chance for the sake of our father's happiness. What annoyed me most about Margo when I first met her was how genuinely nice she was. She had been so kind and respectful of my feelings. I knew Margo had played a huge role in helping my father heal. As much as I had wanted to hate her, I couldn't.

After they were engaged, Margo sold her house, and Dad sold ours so we could all make a fresh start. They found a house with more space for all of us. It had meant my brothers had to share the basement for their room, but they didn't mind. It was hard to lock up our old house for the last time because there had been so many memories inside. We hoped to take with us only the good memories and leave the bad ones behind.

Chapter 5

The electrician arrived while we were getting ready for lunch. He was doing Bob a favor by working on a Sunday afternoon. Bob took him to the basement while everyone else went to the kitchen to eat. I wasn't really hungry, so I went to the library to look around.

The library was actually a ballroom. The wall on the right side of the room was full of bookcases that stretched from the floor to the tall ceiling. A rolling ladder rested against the shelves on one side. There were two antique striped armchairs and a matching small sofa facing the shelves. Centered on the left wall was a grand fireplace with star-shaped details on the mantel. The back wall was made up almost entirely of large windows and doors with a view of the ocean.

The floor looked different than it did in the rest of the house. It was still hardwood, but instead of straight boards it had an intricate star-shaped pattern of darker and lighter shades of wood that matched the mantel. It was a floor made for dancing. I looked around the room and imagined a time of grand parties and elegance.

Bo startled me when he spoke. I hadn't heard him come in through the swinging door from the dining room.

"This room was made for dancing," he said. He hugged me and spun me around. "All we need is music."

We had slow danced at Dad and Margo's wedding. The difference back then was when he had touched me I hadn't felt like I could melt into a puddle on the floor. What was happening with us?

"I didn't realize you liked to dance so much," I said. "You stepped on my toes last time."

"I never said I was any good at it."

I laughed. "True," I said. I would have gladly let Bo step on my toes again.

Bo still had his arms around me. "I really have missed you," he said. His face was close to mine.

We stared at each other for a moment until a loud noise startled us. Bo let go of me as the electrician walked in through the noisy pocket doors from the front parlor, followed by Bob and my dad. The electrician flipped the light switches and made a few notes on his clipboard. Then he pulled out a tool and stuck it in the outlets on the internal wall and made a few more notes.

Dad looked at Bo and me. "Caroline, hon, you need to go eat," he said. "Margo left a sandwich out for you."

"Okay," I said. I glanced back at Bo as I left the room. I was sorry we had been interrupted because for a moment, I had thought he was going to kiss me. I realized I had wanted him to.

The electrician finished up while I ate alone at the dining room table. When he left, so did Bo and his family. They invited us to attend church with them that evening, but Dad declined and said we would go to the Christmas Eve service with them later in the week. I was disappointed because I had wanted to spend more time with Bo.

We all sat in the living room and discussed our strategy for going through the items left behind in the house. There was so much to do, and we only had two weeks to get it done. We talked about what could be discarded and what needed to be looked over more closely. Margo was eager to help but wanted to make sure she didn't throw out anything that might have value to us. A dumpster and a storage container would be delivered the next day. The local antique store would come after Christmas to collect any items we wanted to sell.

We decided all clothing in the house should be discarded except for Mom's things or anything that might have historical value. Any unnecessary items in the kitchen would be sold or donated. Books would be left alone until we could look through them for any family records before deciding which would be kept and which would be donated to the library. All photographs or portrait paintings would be saved for sentimental value or potential decorations for the B&B. The furniture was to stay where it was except the third floor. Dad had decided we would not rent out the third floor, but rather keep it locked for storage. Any other furniture would be sold to help pay for renovations.

Margo and Trini started in the kitchen. Dad took Brad and Jack to the boathouse. Jon and I went to the stable. I was excited to get to explore something. We were supposed to get more wood to put in the basement after we finished going through the tools. Time was a factor in our work because we only had a few hours of daylight left.

As Jon and I walked inside the stable, I detected the faint scent of hay. Jon walked along the side wall and opened the windows above the stalls so we could see. He took some boxes to the back wall where all the tools were hanging and opened the back door to let in more light.

I looked around while I waited for my eyes to adjust. There were several horse stalls along the left wall with gates made of weathered redwood that matched the siding. Newer hay lined the bottoms of them. The scent of the hay became stronger as a breeze from outside blew through the stable. I looked up at the large rectangular beams supporting the roof and the loft below them. I wanted to climb to the loft, but I didn't see a ladder leading up to it.

As I studied the loft from below, the breeze stopped. For a moment, the inside of the stable felt warmer, then suddenly the air became much colder all around me, but not because of another breeze. I shivered and felt goosebumps all over my body. I felt like someone was watching me from behind.

I turned around and couldn't believe what I saw. A little girl was standing in the middle of one of the stalls. She was no ordinary girl—she was transparent, and her feet seemed to disappear before they reached the ground. I was so scared I couldn't breathe, much less move or scream.

Jon never turned around as I stood there frozen in my tracks. The girl was incredibly beautiful with hair the most radiant red I had ever seen. I wasn't close enough to determine the color of her pale eyes, but they appeared dull and sad. She wore a grey bonnet and overcoat over a light yellow dress with a white pinafore. She looked like she was from another time.

She looked at me with a puzzled expression on her face as I studied her. I thought she was as surprised to see me as I was to see her. She wasn't threatening me in any way, but I was terrified. Finally, with tremendous effort, I was able to speak.

"Who are you?" I whispered.

Instead of answering, the little girl giggled softly, then vanished without a trace. A chill rushed through my body. It felt the same as when I had first touched the doorknob to my room.

"What are you laughing at?" Jon asked as he turned to face me.

"You heard!" I said.

"Yes," he said with a strange look on his face. "I heard you."

"No," I said. "It wasn't me. It was . . ." I felt extremely lightheaded, and my knees became weak. I began to fall.

"Caroline!" Jon yelled. He ran toward me.

I felt my body hit the ground, but not my head. My eyes were closed, but I still saw flashes of color, like light shining through a prism. I'd had that happen before, right before a migraine. It had happened often enough during the last year that my doctor had given me prescription medicine for the headaches. Before I could fully open my eyes, I saw in my mind what felt like a memory—a man dressed in an old-fashioned tuxedo kneeling above me. When I opened my eyes, I saw my panicked brother looking down at me.

"Are you okay?" Jon asked. "Talk to me!"

"I don't know," I said as I tried to sit up.

Jon stopped me. "Not so fast," he said. "Take it slow. I couldn't wake you up for a minute."

I was able to stand with Jon's help. He took me back into the house and put me on the sofa and propped my feet on a pillow. He left the room and quickly came back with Margo and Trini. Margo was carrying a glass of juice. I was embarrassed they were making such a big fuss of me since I felt better by that point. Trini looked anxious when Margo sent her back to the kitchen to continue sorting silverware. Jon went back to the stable after Margo assured him she would stay with me.

"Margo, I'm fine, really," I said. "I just want to sit up."

"Stay lying down for a little bit longer," she said. "And drink this juice in case it was a blood sugar issue."

"Okay, but I'm fine," I said. I took the glass from her. Actually, I still felt a little dizzy.

"Sweetheart, people who are fine don't usually pass out for no reason," she said as she felt my forehead. "No fever. Do you feel nauseated? Does your head hurt?"

I shook my head. I wasn't sick, and my head felt fine, but I began to think I might have been hallucinating. But no, Jon had heard the little girl laugh. She was real. I had seen a spirit—a ghost. The man I saw, was he real? I realized Margo was staring at me.

"Caroline, there's not…is there any possibility you could be pregnant?" she asked.

I immediately sat up to face her, shocked by her accusation. I'd never had a boyfriend. Why would she ask that?

"No, Margo!" I said. "How could you think that? I haven't even kissed a guy yet. I'm not that kind of…no!"

"I'm sorry," she said. "I am so sorry. I didn't think so, but fainting can be an early symptom."

I was reminded of an extremely awkward conversation we'd had not long after she and Dad had gotten engaged. She hadn't been sure if my mother had gotten around to giving me a full talk about sex.

"Just please stop talking about it," I said. "I'm probably crazy, but I'm definitely not pregnant. I know you might not believe me, but—"

"I believe you," she said. "You can trust me."

I reluctantly told her. "I saw something in the stable. A ghost I think. A little girl."

"A ghost?"

"She had red hair and an old-fashioned dress, the kind with a pinafore on it. I could see through her. Then she laughed and disappeared."

Margo placed her hands together as if she were praying and covered her lips with her fingers. She didn't speak for a moment. I began to wish I hadn't told her.

"And Jon didn't see her?" she asked.

"See, I knew you wouldn't believe me," I said. "Jon heard her laugh, but he thought it was me."

Margo looked at me like she understood. "I do believe you, Caroline," she said. "I've experienced something before that I can't explain."

"Like what?"

"It happened right after Steven died," Margo said. She sighed and looked out the window before she continued. "I knew it was coming, but I still wasn't prepared for how everything would just hit me right afterward. I went to the hospital chapel that night after he passed. I was overwhelmed that Jack and Trini had lost their father and I had lost my best friend. I dropped to my knees, cried and begged God to help me find the strength to keep breathing.

"Right after that, I felt someone wrap their arms around me from behind, and they held me for the longest time. I could feel this great burden lift, and I felt at peace for the first time in weeks. When they let go, I immediately opened my eyes and turned around to thank them, but there was no one in sight. Maybe it was God's way of comforting me with an angel or maybe it was Steven. I don't know. But if that's not supernatural, I don't know what is."

"Did anyone believe you?" I asked.

"Do you?"

I nodded and fought back tears.

"I've never told anyone else," Margo said.

All I could do was cry. Margo moved to sit with me on the sofa. I didn't want her to be the right person to help me. I desperately wanted my mother to explain what happened and convince me everything would be okay, but I knew Margo was the right person because of what she had shared with me. That made me even sadder. Mom had never known the same kind of loss Margo had—the kind that came with losing someone too soon. Our shared grief was what had helped me grow to love Margo, rather than the like that had sustained me at first.

"I know it's not fair," Margo said as she hugged me. "This is your mother's house, and she should be the one sitting here with you. My kids and I are intruders in her space."

"It's not that," I said.

But it was.

Chapter 6

I rode into town with Margo and Trini to pick up pizza for dinner. Dad didn't want me left alone in the house, even though I had assured him I felt fine. He and the guys were almost finished packing up the boathouse and the stable. I had spent the remainder of the afternoon resting on the sofa with books I found in the living room. The distraction had helped calm my nerves.

Downtown Bettencourt was decorated for Christmas. All the businesses had festive wreaths, window paint, or lights in their windows. The light posts had blue foil snowflakes attached to their tops.

"Mom, are we going to get a tree?" Trini asked as Margo drove down the main street in town.

"I don't know, honey," Margo said. "I need to talk to Mark first. We have so much to do."

"But, Mom!" she said. "It won't feel like Christmas without a tree!"

"Trini, that's enough! Hush!" Margo said.

Trini was so disappointed I felt like I should speak up. She was right; it wouldn't feel like Christmas without a tree.

"Margo, I don't think Dad would mind," I said. "If we get a real tree and Trini and I make paper decorations, we could burn it all before we go home. Please? Look, there's a tree lot right there."

Margo loudly sighed as she turned into the lot. She knew she was defeated. We picked out a small tree and had it tied to the top of the van within a few minutes. I stayed in the van with Trini while Margo went inside the pizza parlor.

Trini leaned over the back of my seat. "Thank you, Caroline," she said.

"Anytime, kid."

After dinner, I showed Trini how to make paper snowflakes out of pages from the coloring books she had brought with her. We made a paper garland chain to drape on the tree as a finishing touch.

"This is the best night ever!" Trini said. She wrapped her arms around my waist and gave me the biggest hug.

It had been a good night. I had enjoyed spending time with her. Even though we didn't have lights for the tree, it still looked nice in the living room near the front window.

"Caroline, what was your mom like?" Trini asked while we cleaned up our paper scraps.

"She was beautiful and kind like your mother," I said. "She told great stories, and always cooked us breakfast on Sundays before church. She was an accountant, so she was really smart with math and money. When I was your age, she would always braid my hair for me. She loved music and liked to sing along with her records. Even though she said she wasn't any good, I never thought she sang that badly. I miss her a lot."

"Jack misses our daddy too," Trini said. "But I don't remember him. Mom showed me pictures of me and Jack sitting on his lap, but I still can't remember." She looked so small and sad.

"I'm sorry, Trini," I said. "Most people don't have memories from that age. You were so young."

"Mom says he was kind, funny, and strong like Daddy Mark."

"I'm sure he was."

Trini opened one of her coloring books and colored a Christmas tree picture. I sat down beside her and worked on the other page. It had been several years since I'd colored. It was nice.

"Caroline, do you think Daddy Mark would mind if I just called him Daddy or Dad like you do?" Trini asked.

It seemed like she had been thinking about it for a while. It was my first non-superficial conversation with Trini.

"I think you should ask him," I said. "But I don't think he'll mind. In fact, I think it would make him very happy."

"But what about Daddy Steven?" she asked as tears formed in her eyes. "Would it hurt his feelings?"

My heart ached for her. Sometimes I got so caught up in my own grief I forgot Jack and Trini were dealing with it too. They had been six and two when their father, Steven, had died of cancer. Jack had been a little brat when I first met him, mad at the world. He had settled down after he realized being angry all the time was getting him nowhere. Trini had been clingy and starved for fatherly affection—a daddy's girl without a daddy. I was jealous at first when she began calling my father Daddy Mark. It didn't bother me now, though.

"I don't think so," I said.

I was startled when Margo spoke from the doorway. I wasn't sure how long she had been listening.

"Trini, why don't you go ask Mark now. He's still in the kitchen washing the dishes," Margo said. "I assure you that Steven's feelings would not be hurt."

Trini ran out of the room. Margo looked at our tree, then turned around and smiled at me.

"You've just become her idol," she said.

Trini ran back into the room a moment later and began jumping around as she said, "He said yes! Daddy said yes!" She hugged us both, then ran back out.

Jack stormed in a second later. He crossed his arms and glared at his mother. "Really, Mom? Really?" he asked. "He's not our Dad!"

"Jack…" Margo said.

Jack ran upstairs and slammed the door to his room.

Margo had tears in her eyes. "I didn't mean to hurt him," she said. "I didn't think. I have to go talk to him."

"Let me," I said. "I don't think he'll listen to you right now."

Margo agreed and wiped her eyes.

"Besides," I said. "I'm kind of on a roll here with your kids tonight. Too bad I'm such a mess with everything else."

I went to Jack's room and knocked on the door.

"Leave me alone, Mom," he said. "I don't want to talk to you."

"It's not your mom," I said. "Can I come in?"

"Fine," he said.

He was sitting on the bed facing the wall. He hastily wiped his face with his arm as I closed the door behind me. I sat down beside him and tried to get comfortable on the lumpy mattress.

"Yeah, the bed sucks," he said. He crossed his arms and turned to face me. His cheeks were red and streaked with tears.

"Lots of things do," I said. "But if you want to get into specifics, the fact that my mom and your dad died while they were still in their thirties really sucks."

I got up and stacked wood in his fireplace. I didn't know much about building fires, so I tried to remember and replicate what Jon had done for mine by adding bits of newspaper in between the logs. Before long, I had a small fire going to heat up the room. When I looked back at Jack, he was staring off into space, deep in thought.

"You know," he said. "Sometimes I can't remember what his voice sounded like."

"I'm sorry," I said as I sat down beside him.

The poor kid had so much on his mind. I couldn't imagine forgetting the sound of my mother's voice.

"I feel like I have all these memories of him stored in a box…but it doesn't close right, so every day something falls out. All the stuff I'm supposed to remember for Trini. Does that make any sense?" he asked as he looked at me again.

"It makes a lot of sense," I said.

"It just seems wrong to call another man Dad even if he's as great as your dad," Jack said.

"Trini was worried about that too. She didn't want to be disrespectful to you or your dad, but the fact is, my dad is the only dad she'll ever remember. She was just so young when he died. Margo told her your dad wouldn't mind."

"See, even you call my mom by her name," he said. "Just like your brothers."

"We were a lot older when our mom died," I said. "I was your age. We asked Margo before the wedding if we could continue to call her by her first name. She told us she could never replace our mother and calling her Margo was fine."

"Yeah, Mark said the same thing," Jack said. "He said it again tonight, that he could never replace our dad, but hoped we would grow to love him as much as he loves us no matter what we choose to call him, blah blah."

"He's telling the truth," I said. "He does love you. I do too, little brother." I knew telling Jack I loved him would bring an end to our moment.

"Well, you are kind of weird," he said mischievously. "Fainting, really? Between that and drooling over Bo, I'm not sure how reliable your advice is."

"Goodnight, Jack," I said as I messed up his hair. I got up to leave the room and had almost closed the door behind me when he spoke again.

"I love you too, sis," he said.

Jack was a good kid, but I'd never thought he had much depth. I realized there was a lot more to him than belching and fart jokes.

I went to Jon and Brad's room next and interrupted their conversation.

"Jon," I said. "About your bad dream, spill it."

They both looked at me with concern.

"What dream?" Jon asked.

"No more secrets," I said. "I saw a ghost in the stable today."

Chapter 7

My brothers both stared at me in silence before they looked at each other. Jon looked back at me with pity, like he thought I had lost my mind. Brad seemed like he believed me.

"You saw a what?" Brad finally asked.

"While you were unconscious?" Jon asked.

"I saw a translucent little girl right before I fainted," I said. "A ghost, an apparition, a spirit."

"Translucent?" Brad asked.

"Yes," I said. "As in see-through. That laughing you heard, Jon, it was her."

"That's not possible," Jon said. "I know I heard you." Jon was skeptical by nature, just like Dad.

"It's that little girl who died with the owners," Brad said as he snapped his fingers out in front of himself and tried to remember. "That big tragedy Mom told us about. Caroline Marshall's parents died a few months after she did. It was the stable fire; they died trying to save that little girl they adopted. She's the ghost Mom's grandfather thought was stealing all the pies. Remember?"

"Yes," I said. "The Marshall family experienced a lot of tragedy."

"Those were just stories," Jon said. "Probably made up to keep kids from playing around in the stable."

"Stories based on some truth," I said. "I'm sure there were newspaper records or something that told about the fire and the deaths."

"Yeah," Brad said. "Mom told us about all the things her grandparents heard through the years."

"Exactly," Jon said. "Stuff they heard through the years. Don't you think some things could have gotten exaggerated or confused?"

"Who cares?" I asked. "The point is, I saw something, and it scared me so badly I passed out. Now tell me what you dreamed about. Brad told me he dreamed I fell off the lighthouse."

The color drained from Jon's face. "What?" he asked.

Brad recounted his story from earlier.

"Jon," I said. "Please tell us."

Jon looked at Brad and then back at me. He sighed and then told us. "I keep having the same dream every time I close my eyes," he said. "You are falling from the top of the lighthouse, and I can never get to you in time. It's so dark I can't find where you landed. I always wake up before I can find you."

"Dude, we're having the same dream!" Brad said. "That's weird."

"It's this stupid house and all the stories," Jon said. His face was red, and he was beginning to sound flustered. "We're all just too emotional being here, thinking about her."

"Her?" Brad asked. "Mom or the ghost of Caroline Marshall?"

Jon glared at Brad. "You know I'm talking about Mom," he said.

"Are you saying you don't believe me?" I asked. "Strange things happen sometimes, you know."

Jon spoke slowly and chose his words carefully. "I believe you think you saw something," he said.

"I believe you," Brad said. "You seemed to be having some wicked dreams this morning. You were tossing back and forth."

"Maybe," I said. "Hey, next time, don't grab my foot with your ice-cold hands. That's not a fun way to wake up."

Brad looked confused. "I didn't," he said. "I just shook your shoulder and then gave up when I couldn't wake you."

So it hadn't been Brad who grabbed my ankle. Had I dreamt it? I began to doubt everything.

Later that night, I cleaned my room to see what things could be packed away. I was willing to do almost anything to avoid dwelling on what I had seen earlier. My main concern was lighting the room because I didn't think I could handle being alone in the dark. To feel secure, I had to be able to see what I was doing.

I pulled the lanterns off the walls to fill them with oil. The first few lanterns came down easily, and after I had wiped the globes, they were ready to use. When I got to the last lantern, the one to the left of the bookcase, it was stuck.

Finally, after I pulled with all of my strength, I was able to get it off the wall. I stumbled backward as it came loose. I glanced back at the wall and noticed a hand-sized hole behind where the lantern had been. I stood on the tips of my toes to peer inside with the flashlight and was astonished to find a key. Cautiously, I reached in and pulled out the key by its metal ring, avoiding the sharp metal case that had held the lantern. As I held the key in my hand, my eyes drifted to the trunk at the foot of the bed.

There was only one way to find out. I placed the key in the lock and gave it a quick turn. The lock opened instantly, and as it did, a familiar chill came over me. Without more than a moment of thought, I relocked the trunk and laid the key inside the top drawer of the desk.

I went downstairs to get the lamp oil. I was dying to open the trunk, but even my immense curiosity could not bring me to open it in the dark. The light from the fire wasn't bright enough.

Dad was in the living room studying the contents of the bookcase. "Hey there, kiddo," he said. "You might find a few of these books interesting."

I walked over to him and tried to overcome my chilled feeling. "I read a little *Macbeth* today," I said. "My drama teacher would be proud."

"There's a ton more in the library. Did you look at them earlier or were you too busy looking at Bo?"

"Dad!" I said as blood rushed to my face.

"Just an observation," he said. "He seems to put his hands on you whenever he can."

I didn't know what to say.

"Are you feeling better now?" Dad asked as he touched my chin. "You had me worried."

Evidently, Margo had kept the reason for my fainting secret.

"I'm fine," I said. "I probably just didn't eat enough this afternoon. I'll be okay."

"No more headaches?"

"I'm fine, Dad."

As I looked at the bookcase for the second time, I realized it was identical to the one in my room. I did some quick calculations in my head and figured that my room was directly above the living room. The bookcases had to be stacked straight up. I thought that was strange.

Dad noticed I was studying the room. "All of these old houses have a story to tell," he said. "Just imagine what these walls would tell us if they could talk."

He gave the wall beside the bookcase a tap with the back of his hand. It sounded hollow.

"That explains a lot. No wonder this house is freezing," I said.

"That's normal," he said. "It's an internal wall. Your great-grandparents had new insulation put in most of the exterior walls when they were renovating, but they didn't replace the original windows. We may have to do that before too long."

"Ah," I said. "I think all of my walls must be hollow. My room is still so cold, even with the fire."

"You could bunk with Trini. We've got the oil heater set up for her. It's the only room with no fireplace."

"No, that's okay. Her room is too small anyway. I'll be fine with just an extra blanket."

"I think it was a sewing room when the house was built. I guess it doesn't matter," Dad said. "We'll be converting that room into a bathroom anyway. One bathroom is not going to work for this house. It's been a pain having only one for all seven of us."

Dad would have talked all night, but I was desperate to get back upstairs to the trunk.

"Dad, where's the lamp oil?" I asked.

"Margo put it in the kitchen," he said. "Bob also left us some new wicks. Be careful with the lanterns, they can be tricky. Let me know if you need any help. Your mom never used the one beside the bookcase because it was stuck."

"I managed to get it down," I said.

"Wow," Dad said. "You're stronger than she was. Me too. I could never get it down either."

"Thanks, Dad. Goodnight," I said. I hugged him and then went back upstairs.

I filled the lanterns with oil and returned them to the walls. I saved the hardest one for last. Surprisingly, the last lantern was much easier to put back in place. I lit the lanterns, then tapped the wall beside the bookcase and confirmed it was hollow like the wall in the living room. I checked the other three walls and found that the outside walls were solid. I had hoped to find a way to explain why my room was so much colder than the rest of the house.

The light from the lanterns gave my room a pleasant glow, but the room still felt strange to me. I retrieved the key to the trunk and opened the lid. Once the trunk was open, I was immediately overcome with the sickening aroma of cedar, flowery perfume, and spices I couldn't identify.

I ignored the scent and carefully removed the red and yellow patchwork quilt that covered the trunk's contents. Beneath the quilt was the most beautiful white dress I had ever seen. It was a wedding gown with intricate lace details I could tell were hand-sewn. I carefully placed the dress on my bed to not damage the delicate garment.

Below the dress, a white crocheted blanket was neatly folded beside an old rag-doll. Next, I found a tiny long-sleeved white dress and a matching bonnet with lace details similar to those on the wedding gown; it was a baby's christening outfit. Other baby clothes and a few blankets, all white and plain, filled the bottom of the trunk.

The trunk bottom was made from planks of wood that resembled the thin planks of the hardwood floors in the house. There were two small holes—no bigger than my fingers—on each side that I assumed were for drainage.

As I placed everything back in the trunk exactly how I had found it, I felt an overwhelming sense of sadness. The feeling was still with me when I climbed into bed.

Chapter 8

Visions of the lighthouse haunted my dreams. A few times I woke up feeling frightened but was able to go back to sleep. At one point I woke up and sensed the presence of someone else in the room with me. At first, I thought I was still dreaming, but then realized I could hear what sounded like movement in the darkness. I looked at my fireplace, which had only a few glowing embers left. A shadow passed in front of it and appeared to move toward me.

It was all I could do to scream before a cold hand clamped over my mouth. Within seconds, my brothers were by my side, and I no longer felt the hand or the presence. I was certain at that point I was wide awake. I could see better with the light from their room shining in through my doorway. Brad lit a couple of the lanterns and added more wood to my fire, which gave the room the same warm glow I had enjoyed earlier.

"Caroline?" Jon asked as he placed his warm hands on the sides of my face. "Are you okay?"

I shook my head and burst into tears. I had no idea what was happening to me, and I was terrified.

Brad closed the door. "What happened?" he asked as he returned to my bedside.

Though I was shivering uncontrollably, I wiped the tears off my face and managed to speak. "I was dreaming, and when I woke up, there was someone in here with me."

"What!" Jon said. "There's no way someone could have been in here. Whoever it was would have had to pass us in the hall. Did you see the person?"

"No," I said. "I felt them. They put their hand over my mouth when I screamed before you two got in here. It was another ghost I think."

"It's okay," Brad said. He put his arm around me. "It was only a dream."

"I was awake," I said. "Wasn't I?"

"You only dreamed you were awake," Jon said. "It's happened to me a few times. What was your dream about?"

"I don't remember," I said. "I just remember waking up. How loud did I scream?"

"It wasn't very loud," Jon said.

"I guess no one else woke up," Brad said. "They didn't hear you. We were awake talking."

"Are you okay now?" Jon asked.

"Yeah, I think so," I said. "Just leave the lanterns going, I'll turn them off later."

"Don't go to sleep with them lit," Jon said as they left.

"There's no danger of that," I said. "And I know I was awake."

My brothers went back to their room. Even with the fire, I was still freezing. I went to the closet to get my extra blanket and could hear their voices through the wall. I stayed in the closet for a moment to listen.

"I think this place really is haunted," Brad said. "I felt like someone was watching me while I was in the boathouse."

"In the boathouse with two other people," Jon said. "Dad or Jack could have been looking at you at some point. If you're so sure, why didn't you say anything to Caroline?"

"That's not what I mean. And I didn't want to scare her any more than she already is. Don't you think this place is even the least bit creepy?" Brad asked.

"Well, maybe a little, but you know I don't believe all those ghost stories," Jon said. "It's a load of crap. Everything is probably so distorted. Who knows what's true anymore?"

"You listened," Brad said. "I think you know the stories better than I do."

"My memory is better than yours, and I only listened because Mom was such a good storyteller," Jon said. "Just because I listened respectfully doesn't mean I am as gullible as you and Caroline."

"Says the guy who had nightmares last night," Brad said. "Just admit it bothered you."

"Fine, it bothered me," Jon said. "And then with what happened today, I'm worried about her. You didn't see. She was so pale, and then she just fell down. I barely caught her in time to keep her head from hitting the ground."

"Because she saw a ghost and freaked out," Brad said. "How else would you explain that?"

"Maybe she's getting sick, or maybe she didn't eat enough, and her blood sugar was out of whack or hell, maybe another migraine was trying to start," Jon said. "She hallucinated, plain and simple."

"Yeah, whatever," Brad said. "We'll keep an eye on her. And maybe Bo can distract her. He's a good guy so we won't have to bother killing him."

I listened for a while longer, but they didn't say anything else. I took the blanket back to my bed and turned out the lanterns. The glow from the fire was enough to comfort me so I could attempt to go back to sleep.

Just knowing Brad sensed the eeriness of the house put me at ease, but it was still troubling that something was happening that I didn't understand. Brad had not grabbed my ankle earlier, and no one had actually been in the room with me when I had woken up and felt the hand on my mouth. The only explanation I could think of was the ghost from the stable, or another ghost was trying to communicate with me. Perhaps it was Caroline Marshall.

Mom had told me once her grandmother thought ghosts had unfinished business and could communicate with people who were sensitive. I always thought spirits had to be real. I had never believed everything just stopped when someone died. I had grown up learning about heaven in church and always thought of it as a destination for the soul after death. It made sense to me that some confused souls might get lost along the way. My mother's faith had been so strong I always felt like she knew the way to heaven. I was certain she was there and at peace. Maybe that's what the ghost wanted. Maybe there was something I could do to help her find peace. If only I could stop being afraid.

I picked up my mother's diary off the nightstand and flipped through the pages. I was disappointed that only the first few pages were written on. Mom had been sixteen, about a month away from turning seventeen when she had written the entry. It had been the summer before her senior year in high school.

July 5, 1972

My father tells me that writing things down will improve my grades in English next term. I would much rather tell stories aloud like Granny. She and Gramps let me have a party here for the 4th. I invited Marlene and Bobby. It is still so strange to see them together now. We were all friends for so long. I never thought they would get together someday. They brought along his sister, Serena, and some of their friends from school.

Marlene wanted to set me up with Gary, one of Bobby's friends. Gary was nice, but I had to remind her that I am going steady with Mark Douglas back home. I don't know how things will end up with us, but I do care about him very much. I think I'm in love with him. I miss him this summer. He is back home working and calls me every day that he can.

Serena said she could feel the presence of spirits as soon as she walked in the house. She's gotten so strange as she has gotten older. She wasn't this weird when we were kids playing at the beach all summer. As much as I love listening to the old ghost stories that Granny tells me, I have never seen a ghost here in this house. Gramps says the stable ghost keeps stealing Granny's pies out of the kitchen windowsill, but I think he is just being silly. Why would a ghost need to eat a pie, even if they are as good as Granny's? Would ghosts even need to eat? Honestly, I think Gramps is messing with Granny. He has so much fun with it I just play along. I am not saying that ghosts don't exist. I just haven't seen any evidence. Granny says you have to be sensitive, so maybe I'm not sensitive.

There I go, rambling on. Anyway, back to Serena. She convinced everyone that we should hold a séance. I had to get out the dictionary to know how to spell it. We lit the lanterns in my room and took some of the candles Gramps had in the kitchen. I had to close all of the windows *and shutters except for a small bit because a storm was rolling in. We could hear the thunder and see the lightning even though the rain had not started yet.*

We held hands and sat in a circle in front of the fireplace and Serena said some weird chants trying to contact the spirit of Caroline Marshall. Nothing happened. The wind blew out all the lanterns and some people downstairs screamed when the power went out, but other than that the night was uneventful. Everyone in my room was acting strange afterward. I think the storm had them spooked.

After everyone had gone home when the storm ended, I went to bed and had the strangest dream. I was lying in bed and could feel my stomach large and hard with movement inside it. I dreamed I was pregnant I guess. I didn't feel happy in the dream. I felt a sense of dread. It was so strange.

I think I do want children someday, two or maybe three. I don't want them to be alone like I am without a brother or sister. I want a house full of fun and laughter, and if I have a daughter, I will name her Caroline. Maybe it's silly to want to name my possible future child after a long-dead relative who died young so long ago, but I love the name. It's so beautiful and sounds like a lullaby when I say it.
-Roberta

I flipped through the diary again and hoped to find another entry, but there were none. Hot tears stung in my eyes. I hugged my knees and thought about my mother and the owner of the trunk who must have died long ago. Then I cried myself to sleep.

Chapter 9

December 23, 1996

I woke up feeling refreshed. More than anything, I hoped my brothers had forgotten about the night before. I was embarrassed for screaming like I had. Luckily, no one else had heard, or if they had heard me, they didn't mention it. It was better that way since I was still trying to process everything myself.

I was determined to figure out what the stable ghost wanted. After all, she hadn't tried to harm me. Maybe she just needed someone to listen to her, if I could just stop being afraid.

Dad and Margo decided to go shopping for a few Christmas presents to put under the tree. I had hoped they would take Jack and Trini with them so I could explore more of the house by myself, but I was left in charge of them for the morning.

As soon as Dad and Margo left, I put the kids to work on their chores. I began to wash the breakfast dishes so I could keep an eye on Trini, who was supposed to be sweeping the floor. She was dancing around in her sock feet with the broom more than she was working.

"Trini!" I called to her from the kitchen. "Be careful, these old floors are slippery!"

"Don't worry, I'll be very careful!" she said.

As I filled the sink with water, I watched through the window while my brothers and Jack shoveled snow away from the path to the storage container and dumpster. It was a warmer day than usual, so everything looked grim and mushy in the sunlight. Dripping water was forming icicles along the roofline of the small back porch.

Just as I put my hands in the sink, the phone rang. I called for Trini to answer it while I continued to wash the dishes. She came in the kitchen a few seconds later.

"It's Bo," she said. "He wants to talk to you."

She took the phone's receiver off the wall, stretched its long cord across the kitchen, and placed it on my shoulder.

"Hey, Bo," I said.

"Caroline? Where's Jon?" he asked. He sounded confused.

"Trini said you wanted to talk to me."

"I was trying to get Jon," Bo said. "Trini said he was outside. I thought she was going to get him."

"So you don't want to talk to me?" I asked as I joked with him. "That hurts."

Bo laughed. "I always want to talk to you," he said. "I just have a question for Jon."

"What is it then?" I asked.

"Well, I talked to him about meeting my cousin, Justice. I think they might get along. I wanted to make sure he was still willing to do that. She and I are going to the beach tonight with a few of our friends," Bo said. "There'll be a bonfire and everything. I was calling to see if you guys wanted to go."

From what Bo had told me about Justice, I seriously doubted she and Jon would get along. I knew she was a little older than my brothers since she had just graduated high school in the spring. Justice seemed like more of a free spirit and was definitely more open-minded than Jon. She took great pride in being an expert on the town's most famous ghost stories and legends. But maybe Bo saw some compatibility that I didn't.

"It sounds like fun," I said. "I have to ask my dad."

"Great. Just let me know. And ask—"

We were interrupted by a thud followed by the crash of breaking glass from the living room.

"I have to go," I said. "I'll call you later."

I ran to the living room and found Trini with a guilty look on her face. She glanced down at the floor at a shattered porcelain box that had been sitting on the wall table.

Seeing the broken pieces reminded me of something that had happened the same night Mom had died. Brad had been so upset he'd bumped the table beside the front door as he ran outside. A picture frame from the table had shattered and covered the floor with glass. I had picked up the larger pieces, and in my shock had not realized the glass had cut my hands. I had only noticed when Becca arrived and saw the blood running down my arms while I swept up the remaining glass. Becca's mom, who was also my doctor, had bandaged my hands. I didn't think Dad had ever received a bill for those services. I still had tiny scars on the palms of my hands.

"Damn it, Trini!" I said as I gritted my teeth with frustration more than anger.

"I'm sorry," she said as tears spilled over her cheeks. "It was an accident."

"Go outside," I said. "Right now."

"But it's cold out there," she said.

I glared at her. "You have two seconds to get out of my sight," I said. "Go!"

Before I could even think, she was outside and Jon was inside. I felt terrible for yelling at Trini. Jon told me he would clean up the mess and sent me outside for more firewood. I was already getting tired of lugging wood inside from the stable.

Trini approached me as soon as I got outside.

"I am really sorry, Caroline," she said. She barely spoke above a whisper. "I really didn't mean to."

"Don't worry about it," I said. I pulled Trini into my arms for a hug. "I know it was an accident."

"You do?" she asked. Her eyes looked brighter as she looked up at me.

"Just go help Brad and Jack," I said. "Everything's fine. I'm sorry. I shouldn't have yelled at you."

She hurried off as I walked to the stable. I took slow and deliberate deep breaths hoping the cold air would calm my nerves. I opened the door cautiously, worried about what I might see. I left the door wide open and walked to the stack of firewood. I looked all around me but saw nothing. Before I could turn around with the armload of firewood I had gathered, my skin tingled, and the air around me instantly felt colder.

"What do you want?" I asked.

I turned around and found the little girl standing in the same place as the day before. She illuminated the stall around her.

"Caroline, where have you been?" she asked. Her voice was high-pitched and child-like.

I gasped and dropped the wood at my feet. How did she know my name? I closed my eyes and then opened them again, but this time, she did not disappear.

"Who are you?" I asked. I felt like I might faint again, but was determined to stay alert.

She moved toward me, and I stepped backward to get farther away. I couldn't take my eyes off of her.

"You are dressed oddly," she said. "He is waiting."

"Who are you?" I asked again. I was feeling less afraid of the little girl since I felt like I might be able to help her. If only I could understand what she wanted to tell me. "Who is waiting? Where?"

"Are you mad?" she asked.

She thought I was crazy. I couldn't answer her. Maybe I was crazy. It was one thing to believe in ghosts, but seeing one was a different matter entirely. I blinked several times to see if she would disappear again, but she remained in the same place.

"I am Virginia. He is waiting."

She vanished as a cold breeze hit my face.

Jack spoke from just outside the door. "Need any help?" he asked.

I nearly jumped out of my skin. "Jack! Don't sneak up on people like that!" I said.

"Sorry, I didn't mean to scare you," he said.

"It's fine," I said. I tried to regain my composure, but my voice was shaking. I tried to play it off as being cold. "It's freezing in here. Come help me take in the wood."

Although I had my breathing under control before I got back to the house, I couldn't fool my brother. Jon always knew when something was bothering me. He had everything picked up when I got inside. I was there just in time to see him put a small book back on a hidden shelf underneath the table. I decided to worry about that later because I was far more upset about the ghost in the stable.

Jon helped Jack and me stack the wood beside the fireplace in the living room. I knew we needed a bit more and was relieved when Jack went back by himself to get it. After Jack had left, I realized Jon was looking at me.

"You're not one to get so upset over broken decorations," he said. "You look like you're about to cry."

"Jon, really, I'm fine," I said. "It's just all this old stuff. Nothing can be replaced."

"It's only one box that probably came from a dollar-store when Mom's grandparents lived here," he said. "It's nothing to get so upset about."

I sat down beside the wall and pulled my knees up to my chest. "Now that we're here, I don't want to leave," I said. "I feel close to her here."

"To Mom?" Jon asked.

It was strange that his question caught me off guard. I didn't answer him right away.

Jon raised his eyebrows. "You said you feel close to her here. You're talking about Mom?" he asked.

I nodded. He looked at me for a long time before turning to leave the room, but then stopped and turned back to me.

"Look," he said. "Whatever you're not telling me, I hope you'll tell me when you're ready."

"I just can't tell you I'm crazy until I know for sure," I said. I had to look at the floor to avoid his eyes. I knew I would cry again if I looked at him. How could I tell him what I had seen when I knew he wouldn't believe me?

"I can deal with that," he said. "Don't worry too much about Mom's stories. They're all make-believe. When you're dead, you're dead."

His words stuck with me. I was worried Dad wouldn't believe me either. If ghosts didn't exist, then what had I seen in the stable and what had Brad experienced in the boathouse? What had touched me? I had to figure out what was going on. My sanity depended on it.

Chapter 10

Dad and Margo returned not long after lunch with their arms bulging with presents and a few bags of groceries. I was immediately surprised by how angry Margo was with Trini when she found out what had happened.

"Trini Louise!" she said. Her tone was harsh and stern. "This better not ever happen again. We are guests in this house, and I expect you to respect it. Do you understand me?"

Trini sank back against the wall. "Yes ma'am," she said.

Margo pointed upstairs. Trini walked up the stairs slowly and pouted the whole way. As soon as Trini was out of sight, Margo turned to my father and me and apologized again.

"It's not a big deal, Margo," I said. I felt sorry for Trini. "It was an accident. She only broke an old dollar-store box. It wasn't worth much."

Dad smiled at me. "See there," he said. "Everything's going to be just fine."

My brothers and I talked to Dad about the trip to the beach while he and Margo placed the presents under the tree. Dad was less concerned than Margo about letting us go.

"A bonfire on the beach when there's snow on the ground?" Margo asked. "Is that such a good idea?"

"It'll be fine," Dad said as he tried to reassure her. "There are fire pits the city built especially for it back when I was in college. Roberta and I went several times. It's fairly warm by the fire. The pits are far away from the water, and it's all out in the open where the police patrols can see everything that's going on. At least that's how it used to be. We had to rent out the spots weeks in advance because they were so popular."

"It's still the same way," Jon said. "Bo said the police are all over town making sure nothing crazy is going on. It's just a couple of miles from his house."

"We're just going to hang out and cook hot dogs and roast marshmallows," Brad said. "Tell a few ghost stories."

Jon rolled his eyes. "Sure," he said. "It'll be fun to get out of this house for a while and meet Bo's friends."

Margo looked at us and sighed, finally convinced it was okay for us to go. Jack was disappointed he hadn't been invited. Margo wouldn't have let him go anyway. She said someone his age had no business hanging out with a bunch of kids so much older. Dad agreed and said I was only able to go because my older brothers were going with me. At my age, I wasn't allowed to go out unless it was with a group. Dad allowed dating at sixteen. It occurred to me I would probably be the youngest person at the beach.

Dad gave us the standard speech he used when he let us go out at home. "No drinking, no drugs, and no other morally questionable behavior."

Brad laughed. "Yeah, Dad," he said. "Sounds like a blast—drunken sex on the beach in the snow."

"Get out of here," Dad said as he pretended to slap Brad on the back of the head. "Be back by midnight. Look out for your sister and keep an eye on Bo." He winked at me.

Blood rushed to my cheeks. Jack started laughing. The fact that I liked Bo seemed to be obvious to everyone.

Getting dressed by lantern light was easy, but putting on make-up was more difficult. I had never worn much, mainly foundation, pressed powder and just a hint of lip-gloss. I had to use the mirror in the bathroom for that. My excitement caused me to be ready to go long before we would need to leave. I was willing to do just about anything to get out of the house for a little while and see Bo again. He seemed excited when I called him to let him know we were coming.

While I was waiting for my brothers, I sat in the kitchen with Margo while she cooked dinner for everyone else.

"You be very careful, Caroline," she lectured. "Stay close to your brothers. I want you to take my phone with you so you can call Bo's parents if something goes wrong since we won't have another vehicle here."

"Okay," I said. "You're starting to sound like Dad."

"Well, there are a lot worse things in the world than that," she said. She covered her mouth with her hands. "I'm always saying the wrong thing. I didn't mean to imply—"

"I know," I said.

She hadn't meant to remind me about Mom. I never needed to be reminded. We continued our tasks without speaking. I was relieved when she finally broke the silence.

"I really am sorry about the way Trini behaved today," she said.

"She didn't mean to," I said. "Surely I broke stuff like that when I was a kid."

Margo smiled. "And to think, it wasn't that long ago," she said. "You have grown up a lot since I met you, and into a beautiful young lady."

I laughed. "This is starting to sound a lot like an after-school special," I said.

"Maybe that's a good thing," Margo said as she tossed me a package of French bread to slice.

"Margo, how old were you when you met Steven?" I asked as I spread butter on the bread slices.

She put down the knife she was using to chop lettuce. "Does this have anything to do with Bo?" she asked. She took the pasta off the cooktop and drained it in the sink.

"Maybe a little," I said.

Actually, it had a lot to do with my question. My parents had started dating when they were around my age.

"I was about your age, I guess," she said. She didn't look at me and went back to chopping the salad ingredients. "We became friends first when his family moved to town and then after high school graduation we became more than that."

I had put the bread in the oven and was watching it close-ly. Margo had piqued my interest telling me Steven had been her friend first.

"Just like that?" I asked. I had to quickly get the bread out of the oven to keep it from burning under the broiler.

"Just like that," she said. Her eyes looked distant. "He picked me up from work—I worked at a grocery store—and we got into an argument in the parking lot. I was on edge be-cause I had just broken up with my boyfriend a week or so before then. Steven had locked his keys in his car, and I was upset we would be late for my best friend's engagement party. He got a hanger from the dry cleaner to unlock the door, but by then it was raining. He managed to get it unlocked, and we both looked like drowned rats when we showed up at the party. I was still so mad at him when he took me home later."

I could imagine what Margo must have looked like after a night like that. Her hair was so curly it must have been a nightmare to deal with after getting rained on.

"My parents were out of town, so he walked me to my door," Margo said. "Then I discovered my keys weren't in my purse. After the night I'd had, I just wanted to go inside and go to bed, so I kind of flipped out over everything from the whole night. I started crying about how embarrassing it had been to go to my friend's party looking like a crazed poodle and how the night wasn't getting any better. He told me that I never looked more beautiful and kissed me. It took me by surprise. I think I always loved him, but I didn't know until that kiss I loved him in a romantic way. We had our own engagement party by the end of the summer right before I started college. A lot of people got married right out of high school back then."

"Mom and Dad started dating in high school," I said. "They were so young. It seems weird to be going out with who you're going to marry before you can even drive a car."

"Yes, but you don't always know at the time if the person you're dating is the one," Margo said as she wiped a stray tear from her eye. "Your dad and I were both very blessed to have had that kind of love so young. That's not the norm anymore. I think it's part of why we connected so well when we met. We both had that in common, and neither of us thought we could love someone else again."

Margo and Dad must have been so lonely before they met. I felt even more like a brat for the way I had behaved when they first started dating. I decided to steer the conversation back to me since Margo seemed so sad after talking about Steven.

"Bo's acting like he could think of me as more than a friend," I said. "At least, Jon and Brad seem to think so."

"There did seem to be something going on with the way he hugged you Saturday night," Margo said. "Your dad noticed too. And you do talk on the phone with him a lot."

Dad and Margo had discussed us? It was humiliating.

"He's my best friend," I said. "I like talking to him."

"But how do you feel about him right now after seeing him again for the first time in more than a year?" she asked.

"Confused," I said. I was admitting it to myself as much as I was to her. "I haven't thought of Bo like that before. Now, I feel all nervous and stupid around him. I think I like him too."

Margo nodded. "Well, sweetie, I hate to break it to you, but the confusion feels the same whether you're fifteen or thirty-five," she said.

"That's not comforting at all. Shouldn't there be some wisdom with getting older?"

Margo moved closer to me. She put her hands on my shoulders and looked me in the eyes. "Just take things slowly," she said. "If it's meant to be, then it will be. And, Caroline, all those firsts you have to give…you can only give them once so don't throw away those experiences on just anyone. I wish I had waited for a few of mine, one in particular."

"Thank you," I said as I hugged her. I understood what she was trying to tell me, but I hadn't had any opportunities for firsts of my own so far. I appreciated Margo being so honest and not talking me to like I was a little girl, even though I still felt like one sometimes.

I helped Margo put dinner on the table and then bundled up for the trip to the beach. The day had been warmer, but the temperature had dropped again after sunset. I hoped Dad was right that the fire at the beach would keep everyone warm.

Chapter 11

Bo and his friends were already at the beach when we arrived. As soon as he saw our van he came over to greet us. He grabbed my hand and practically dragged me over to meet everyone.

First, he introduced us to his cousin, Justice. She was pretty and tall, with delicate features. Her long jet-black hair seemed to shine in the light from the fire. Justice was a freshman at the same college my parents had attended.

"Hi," she said as she extended her hand. "You can call me Justy, everyone else does. Bo hasn't stopped talking about you."

I shook her hand. "Caroline Mar—Caroline Douglas," I said.

What had just happened there? Jon and Brad introduced themselves and shook her hand as well. Jon held her hand a little longer than Brad did.

"It's so good to meet you all," she said.

No one acknowledged my slip-up, but I still had trouble paying attention as Bo introduced me to his friends. There were two guys, Shawn and Wesley, who were both average height with brown hair. There was one girl, Jennifer, who was petite with chin-length blond hair. I learned Shawn was a senior, and Wesley and Jennifer were juniors like Bo. Their other friends were out of town for the holidays.

The setup at the beach was very nice. There were three fire pits spread out, each with a small lighted pavilion near the parking lot. The other pits, pavilions, and the well-lit playground farther down the beach were empty. We all gathered around the fire, sat on the rocks that surrounded it, and cooked our hot dogs on sticks. Bo asked me to sit beside him on a rock barely big enough for the both of us. I heard the waves crashing in the distance and smelled the salt in the air.

"How can you guys stand to live at that creepy Bettencourt Estate?" Shawn asked. "That place is haunted you know."

"We've all grown up hearing the stories about it," Jennifer said. "Caroline Marshall is a town legend."

"Yeah," Shawn said. "She killed herself and then came back as a ghost and killed her boyfriend, her parents, and that little girl."

"The library has a special section that has all the newspaper articles about deaths of the Marshall family," Justice said. "I helped put it together. I work there in between classes and on Saturdays."

I knew I had to get to the library to see those articles at some point during our trip. I couldn't forget I had almost introduced myself as Caroline Marshall. I didn't even realize I had been thinking about her.

"We're only staying there for a little while," Brad said. "We don't live there. We inherited the place from our great-grandparents."

"Have you guys seen any ghosts?" Jennifer asked.

Jon looked over at me and then shook his head. "No," he said. "We're a little too old for all the ghost stories."

"We looked for her grave in the cemetery on Halloween night. Do you remember, Bo?" Wesley asked.

"I remember," Bo said. "We never did find it."

"Hey," Justice said as she looked at me. "You were named after her, right?"

"Yeah, my mom grew up with the stories and liked the name," I said. "It's kind of weird."

"My mom thinks there's a lot more to the story," Wesley said. "I mean, the boyfriend gets fired, and Caroline was supposed to be married that next summer. Then all of a sudden, she's dead, he's dead, and just about everyone else is dead too. It's weird."

"My mom thinks Caroline was hidden away because she got pregnant," Justice said. "And that's why her wedding was postponed, and Thomas got fired. They hid her away and sold her baby or maybe the baby died. She couldn't handle the grief of losing her child, so she killed herself."

"Seriously?" Bo asked.

"It's one of her new theories," Justice said. "We found the plot records about a month ago. I know where her grave is now. It's close to the Bettencourts. The stone is damaged, worn down. Mom touched the grave and said she felt like Caroline had given birth."

Bo nodded and seemed to understand which grave Justice was talking about.

"A seventeen-year-old having a baby, back then?" Shawn asked.

"I would imagine more seventeen-year-olds had babies back then than they do now," Jennifer said. "People got married younger."

"But she wasn't married," Shawn said.

Jennifer stared at him in disbelief. "Neither are we," she said. "Biology pretty much worked the same back then."

Shawn looked confused, but then he seemed to understand what she was referring to. "Oh," he said.

Everyone laughed. Bo hadn't mentioned that Shawn and Jennifer were seeing each other. I should have figured it out by how close they sat together on a rock similar to the one Bo and I were sitting on.

"She could have just run away with her boyfriend," Wesley said. "They could have gone to another town, and no one would have known they weren't married."

"It was a lot harder to run away back then," Justice said. "In the winter it would have been impossible for a pregnant girl to go off on her own on foot—if she was pregnant."

"My dad went to a séance back in the 70s at the estate," Wesley said. "There was a girl there named Roberta and Dad said the ghost was trying to communicate through her, but a storm interrupted them."

"Roberta was our mother," Jon said. "And that's bullshit. These are all just stories, so distorted nobody knows what's true anymore."

It wasn't like Jon to use that kind of language. I wasn't surprised the séance story upset him more than the other stories. No one said anything for a little while, so I assumed Bo had told his friends about our mother's accident even if he hadn't told them her name.

"There's no proof she actually killed herself. Where's the note? What if it was an accident?" Jennifer asked. "Maybe Caroline went to the top of the lighthouse for some reason, but then she fell. Whatever happened, it's sad she died when she was so young. I mean, she was our age, it's tragic."

It was tragic that anyone had to die so young. I had to get away from everyone because all the talk made me think about my mother. The last thing I wanted to do was cry in front of Bo's friends. I got up and walked to the closest pavilion. The cold air was enough to keep my tears away. I sat down at the picnic table. I felt the cold metal bench through the back of my coat. My brothers called my name, but Bo followed me.

"Hey," Bo said. "I'm sorry, I didn't know they would bring up your mom." He sat down beside me and put his hand on my knee.

"I'm okay," I said. I was more embarrassed than upset at that point. Everything that had happened over the past couple of days had caught up with me.

"Do you want to be alone for a bit?" he asked.

I shook my head and wiped the tears from my eyes. He was the only person I wanted to talk to. I wanted to talk to my friend Bo who I could always talk to on the phone. I could always tell him anything.

"What's going on?" he asked as he hugged me. "You know you can tell me anything."

It didn't help that he when he hugged me my skin tingled. I had to get my attraction to him under control so I could think straight.

"I don't know," I said. "I'm either going crazy, or I am seeing and feeling a ghost at the house. Possibly more than one."

Bo didn't even flinch when I told him. He reached out and held my hand. He had taken off his gloves, and I could feel the warmth of his hand through my gloves. The way he diagonally intertwined his fingers with mine was distinctive and familiar. It was the same way he had held my hand at my mother's funeral. How could I have forgotten it was him?

"Have you told anyone else?" Bo asked. "What happened?"

"I told my brothers and Margo. Jon thinks I hallucinated since I fainted right after I saw a little girl in the stable. I felt someone in my room last night. Someone different I think. They put their hand over my mouth."

"To hurt you?" he asked. He seemed genuinely concerned. "You can't stay there."

"No, not to hurt me, to stop me from screaming, I guess. They haven't tried to hurt me. I just don't know what they want. I saw the little girl a second time today. She knew my name and said he was waiting for me, but disappeared before she could tell me who. She told me her name was Virginia. I haven't told anyone about that. She said I was dressed oddly. She thought I was crazy when I asked her who she was."

"Virginia?" Bo asked. His eyes were wide. "That's the name of the little girl who died in the stable when it burned down. Justice told me about it. The Marshalls were taking care of Virginia. Thomas was her older brother. She didn't know your name; she thought you were Caroline Marshall."

"His sister!" I said. I turned sideways on the bench so I could face Bo. "Mom never told me that."

"She probably didn't know. A lot of the newspapers were just recently converted to film to preserve them. I doubt she had access to them when she lived here," he said. "Living in this town, I believe in ghosts. I believe you saw one and I don't think you're crazy at all. I'd freak out too."

"What am I going to do?" I asked. "I'm afraid. Crap. She thinks I'm the other Caroline, so that means she was telling me that Thomas is waiting for me. Is his ghost coming after me next?"

Bo squeezed my hand. "You just have to figure out what they want," he said. "I'll help you, and we'll get Justy and Aunt Serena to help too. I promise we'll figure this out."

When I looked back at the fire, I could see Jon was in a heated argument with Justice. I could hear their voices but was too far away to understand what they were saying. Jon's skepticism was unparalleled.

"Is she always like that?" I asked.

Bo turned around to look. "No," he said as he laughed a little. "Sometimes she likes to argue with people."

He was still holding my hand. He looked like he had a million thoughts running through his head, but he didn't say anything. I wanted to kiss him so badly I could almost imagine taking a chance and just going for it.

"You know, my dad didn't want me to be alone with you," I said as I bumped Bo's shoulder with my own. "He told my brothers to watch out for me and to keep their eyes on you."

I had given him an opening. *If he does have feelings for me, maybe he'll do something,* I thought. *Boys are supposed to initiate a kiss, right?* Becca's boyfriend had kissed her first.

"That's funny," Bo said with a warm smile. "I hope he knows I'd never hurt you. You're like family to me."

With that comment, I felt like the whole world came crashing down around me. I pulled my hand out of Bo's grip and placed both hands in my pockets to keep them warm.

Everyone had misread Bo's feelings for me. I was heartbroken and disappointed, but I couldn't let it show. My feelings for him were so much stronger than I had realized. *I have to put this out of my mind*, I told myself. *He is still my friend—my best friend.*

I smiled and tried hard not to cry. "Oh, he was only kidding," I said. "He knows you're like a brother to me."

"Like a brother?" Bo asked. He sounded disgusted. "God, I hope not!"

My feelings were all mixed up. I went from wanting to kiss him to wanting to punch him in the face.

"You have me all confused!" I said. I stood up to walk away. I was so ready for the conversation to be over I didn't care what I said anymore. "I don't know what to say to you. You look at me the way you do and then tell me I'm like family, so I agree with you, and then you disagree. What do you want me to say? You don't make any sense!"

Bo looked as confused and frustrated as I felt. He stood up, threw his arms out to his sides, and turned away from me.

"You're the only one who makes any sense to me at all right now!" he yelled as he turned to face me again.

He had never yelled at me before. We'd never had an argument at all—not even a petty squabble during a board game when we were kids.

"What the hell are you talking about?" I asked. I was so irritated with him my whole body felt warm. I took off my hat and threw it on the table.

Bo moved so close to me I had to push against his chest and take a step back to see his face. I was frightened of him for a moment. He seemed desperate to say something but acted like he might choke on his words if he tried. His mouth was clamped tight, and his nostrils flared with each breath.

Suddenly, he grabbed the sides of my face, pulled me forward and kissed me. I instinctively closed my eyes, but other than that I had absolutely no idea what I was doing when I kissed him back. He wrapped one arm tightly around me and held me close to him, which trapped my arms in between us. I wouldn't have known what to do with my arms anyway. I must have screamed a hundred times in my mind because I couldn't believe what was happening.

Everything around me stopped—all sounds and all sensations except for the softness of his lips against mine, and the exhilaration I felt all the way down to my toes. When he pulled away, I was afraid to open my eyes because I thought I was dreaming.

When I opened my eyes and tried to speak, I couldn't. I was so short of breath I must have forgotten to breathe the whole time. One of his hands was still on my face, and I couldn't look away from his eyes. I had never seen blue eyes as beautiful as his. *I guess he has feelings for me after all,* I thought.

"I'm sorry," Bo said as he placed both hands on my shoulders. He was short of breath too. "For yelling at you, and I shouldn't have done that without asking first. Forgive me?"

"No, it's okay," I said. I stayed close to him.

My lips felt numb and used. My arms were still resting against Bo's chest. I could feel his heart beating as fast as mine. I felt like I had just gotten off of a roller coaster. It took all of my energy to slow my breathing.

Bo seemed to be struggling in the same way. His hands were shaking when he let go of me to put on his gloves. "We should go back to the fire," he said. "It's getting colder. I think we'll have to go home soon. You're shivering."

He took off his blue wool scarf and wrapped it around me. I pulled it tighter around my shoulders and put the ends up to my face. It smelled like him. He picked up my hat off the table and slipped it onto my head. I felt like a child getting helped by a parent, but I put that out of my mind. The thought of leaving the beach made me sad.

Everyone was still talking when we rejoined them by the fire. Brad looked up at us, but no one acted like they had seen us kiss.

"It's probably the cemetery that's haunted," Shawn said. "The ghosts want headstones."

"The cemetery is sacred ground; it can't be haunted, it's right beside a church," Jennifer said.

"That's not necessarily true," Justice said. "There have been documented sightings."

"I think you're all too easily influenced by these stories," Jon said.

"And you're too skeptical, Jon. Open your mind," Justice said as she pointed to her temple. "Have we not told you enough? There's some freaky shit that happens in this town. Wait until you see the lights in a few days. It happens every year after Christmas."

"And if I do," Jon said. "I'm sure it can be rationally explained."

"So you really don't believe you're staying in a haunted house?" Shawn asked.

"I haven't seen any evidence that ghosts exist," Jon said. "I'm not saying Caroline Marshall didn't exist. We know she did, we're descendants of her sister. I just don't believe that she or anyone else is haunting the lighthouse."

"You'll believe when you feel it," Brad said. "There is definitely something going on at the estate."

Jon gave up at that point. It was time for us to leave anyway. We all said our goodbyes. I didn't know what to say or how to behave with Bo as we stood beside my brothers. I thought about giving him back his scarf, but I wanted to keep something of his close to me.

"I'll call you tomorrow," Bo said as he grabbed just the tips of my fingers.

"Okay," I said as I smiled at him.

I noticed Brad was smirking at me. He knew.

Chapter 12

Brad drove on the way back. I sat in the front with him, and Jon sat in one of the back seats and quietly stared out the window. I was grateful to have the heater blowing directly in my face.

"So, what's up with you and Bo?" Brad asked. He didn't take his eyes off the road. "That was some kiss."

I was relieved it was too dark for them to see my face because I knew it was bright red.

"What!" Jon said.

With the light from a passing car, I saw that Jon was smiling as much as Brad.

"Oh, you missed it," Brad said. "You were too busy sparring with Justy. She's feisty and gorgeous; you should go for it, bro."

"She's cute, but we don't get along, and it's not practical," Jon said, quickly dismissing Brad's suggestion. "Caroline, you kissed Bo?"

"He kissed me," I said.

"Hmm," Jon said. "Never thought he'd be bold enough to make the first move. I thought it would have to be you. Go Bo."

Brad laughed so hard I thought he might drive off the road. "Oh he went," he said. "It was all romantic-comedy style. They were arguing—kind of like you and Justy were—and then Bo just grabbed our baby sister and kissed her. That's why Wesley said 'It's about damn time' because apparently Bo never shuts up about Caroline."

"I didn't hear him," Jon said.

"Again, you were in a pretty intense argument with Justy," Brad said. "The rest of us were watching Caroline and Bo."

"Guys, just let it go," I said. "And please, please don't tell Dad." I was mortified that almost everyone had seen us.

"My lips are sealed, even if yours weren't," Brad said.

Jon laughed. I glared at him.

"I hate you both," I said as I buried my face in my hands.

"Sorry! Sorry, last one I promise," Brad said. "You two are cute together, and his friends think so too."

I had to change the subject, or they would have teased me all night. "I saw the ghost in the stable again today," I said. "This time she talked to me. Her name is Virginia."

"Like the state name?" Brad asked.

"Yes," I said. "She said 'he is waiting' like she thinks I'm Caroline Marshall and Thomas is waiting for me. Bo said Thomas was her brother."

"I don't understand," Jon said.

"People die tragically," Brad said. "They don't go into the light. They haunt. What the hell is so difficult to understand?"

Jon sighed. "Then where the hell is Mom?" he asked. "Her death was pretty damn tragic!"

It felt like a bomb had gone off in the van. None of us said anything for a minute or two. I was stunned, but it made sense. Jon didn't believe in ghosts because he thought if Mom wasn't one then they couldn't possibly exist. I had never thought about ghosts like that because I had always believed in the possibility.

Brad finally broke the silence. "Oh my God!" he said. "What the hell is wrong with you? Mom wouldn't haunt us.

She would want us to move on and for Dad to be happy again."

"She's in heaven, Jon, at peace," I said. "I'm sure of it."

Jon wouldn't look at me and didn't speak the rest of the drive back. I gave him his space and continued talking to Brad.

"Bo said he could get his aunt to help me," I said. "To figure out what's going on and help the ghost or ghosts move on."

"That's great," Brad said. "While you and Bo were busy, Justy told us her parents were at the séance too and that something creepy happened. Maybe her mom, Serena, can tell us more about it. I think there's more to the story than what Wesley said."

"There is. I found a diary Mom wrote in. She wrote about the séance and said everyone was acting weird after it was over, but she didn't really think anything had happened. What if something did happen and she just couldn't remember?"

"Sounds possible," Brad said as he turned in the driveway.

The tunnel of trees looked even more frightening than it had the first time I'd seen it. By the time we got to the front of the house, a chill had settled over my entire body. Just as I was about to open my door, Jon finally spoke again.

"I found something today when I was cleaning up that you should see," he said.

"What did you find?" I asked. I remembered the book I had seen him put under the table in the living room.

"I found a photo of a teenage girl who looks just like you, Caroline," Jon said. "It looks ancient—like those metal photos you see in museums."

"Looks like her?" Brad asked.

"Practically identical," Jon said.

"How is that possible?" I asked. I had found my own skepticism. "Jon, you're scaring me."

"I'm scaring myself," he said. "I don't want to believe any of this."

As soon as we got inside the house, Jon showed us the photograph. What I had seen him put away earlier wasn't a book at all. It was a small leather case covering a frame. The photo appeared shiny and metallic underneath the glass. The young woman in the photo was wearing the dress I had found in the trunk in my room. Her expression was solemn, and her dark eyes looked sad. Her light hair was in an elaborate braided bun piled on top of her head. I studied her face and found it remarkably similar to my own.

"It's like looking in a mirror," I said.

"Who is this?" Brad asked. "How old is it?"

I looked at the back of the case and quickly calculated the Roman numerals MDCCCXLVI. I had always thought Roman numerals were interesting.

"1846," I said as I pointed to the stamp on the back of the case. "It says it right there beside the portrait studio copyright."

"Take it out," Brad said. "See if there's a name on the photo."

"No, we can't," I said. "That could damage it. I think it's one of those daguerreotype photos I learned about in my journalism class. They scratch easily."

"Maybe it's Bonnie," Brad said.

"It's not Bonnie," I said. "Bonnie would have been already married then. I think this is Caroline. Back then, people took photos or had portraits painted in their wedding gowns months before their weddings. I found this dress in the trunk in my room—her room, along with a bunch of baby clothes she was probably making for Bonnie's baby."

"Or her own," Brad said. "You heard what Justice said."

"Maybe," I said. "I don't know."

"So you look exactly like Caroline Marshall," Brad said. "No wonder the ghost thinks you're her. This is all too weird."

"We don't know for sure who this is," Jon said. "But she was our ancestor, and resemblances like this happen, so I guess it's possible."

"You heard Virginia laugh," I said. "Do you really think I'm crazy or forgot to eat? I've seen her twice now. And someone or something has been in my room and touched me just like I told you."

"I think there was something in her room," Brad said. "The air was so cold beside her bed, but the fire still had a lot of hot embers when I added more wood. The room shouldn't have been so cold."

"No, I don't think you're crazy. It might be me who's crazy," Jon said with a sigh. "I'm really sorry I didn't believe you."

Chapter 13

Christmas Eve, 1996

I was terrified to go to sleep that early morning on Christmas Eve. Before bed, I prayed for peaceful rest and promised whatever spirits were listening that I would try to help them. I just needed more time to process everything. As silly as I felt doing so, I slept with Bo's scarf curled up beside my face so I could continue to smell him.

My dreams were filled with the replaying of the kiss with Bo and other scenes that were as familiar as memories, but not my own. I woke up feeling like I had been dancing, but I could not recall my partner's face. Another face I saw was etched into my mind, a handsome young man with dark hair and the bluest eyes I had ever seen besides Bo's eyes.

It was still early in the morning when I dragged myself out of bed. I dressed in a warm fleece shirt and jeans since I was supposed to work on the third floor. I pulled my hair into a bun to keep it out of my face. As I glanced in the mirror, I thought I looked older somehow.

We still had so much to go through in the house. I didn't wait for anyone else to wake up. I grabbed my flashlight and a box, then headed upstairs. I chose to start in the room directly above mine. Since the sun rose on that side of the house, I knew it would be the brightest room because it had so many windows.

The room was exactly like mine in layout, except for the dormer windows, but had less furniture. The bookcase was identical to the ones in my room and the living room. All three were stacked up on top of each other beside the fire-places in each room. I thought the chimneys had to be con-nected somehow. The bookcase had several large frames stacked against the front and held only one thick book on the top shelf. I had to stand on the tips of my toes and stretch to reach it. I hoped it contained the family records my mother had told me about.

I carefully wiped the dust off the cover of the ivory-colored book, which was a Bible with gold lettering on the front. Inside the front cover, several different styles of elegant cursive handwriting laid out my family history. I sat on the floor beside a window for more light and skimmed through the names and dates. The whole thing was a bit confusing, but I was able to tell how my mother had traced herself back to Bonnie's daughter.

Campbell (d.1840) and Elberta (d.1843) Bettencourt, wed in 1804. Josette born 1805 and Averill born 1808, died 1821.

Josette (d.1847) and Colin (d.1847) Marshall wed 1823. Bonnie born 1826 and Caroline born 1829, died 1846. Virginia adopted 1846 (d.1847)

Bonnie (d.1885) and Weston (d.1879) Brown wed 1845, Weston Jr. (d.1863) born 1846, Antoinette born 1846.

Antoinette (d.1910) and Pierre (d.1904) Heuse wed 1866. Twins Pierre Jr. and Philip born 1870.

Pierre Jr. (d.1910) and Sarah (d.1910) Heuse wed 1891. Pierre III born 1892, died 1910 and Marguerite born 1893. Boy, born 1896, died 1896.

Philip (d.1910) and Liana (d.1910) Heuse wed 1892, Philipa born 1892, Millicent born 1896 died 1910, Patience born 1899 died 1910, Girl died 1901 and Fay born 1903 died 1910.

Philipa (d.1961) and Bellamy (d.1959) Guinard wed 1909. Cadencia born 1910.

Marguerite (d.1911) and Todd McLean wed 1909. Boy died 1911.

Cadencia (d.1980) and Robert (d.1978) Levy wed 1928. Mavis born 1931.

Mavis and Howard Baker wed 1952. Roberta born 1955.

Roberta and Mark Douglas wed 1977. Twins Jonathan and Bradley born 1979.

The records stopped. Mom's grandmother Cadencia had died during August of 1980. I recognized Mom's handwriting from the death date that was written beside Cadencia's name. I loved studying history in school. The fact that my ancestors had cared enough to write down family records for the next generation was truly a treasure. It was sad how many of them had died when they were young.

I used the pen I had brought with me to add the death dates for my grandparents, Mavis and Howard, who had died in 1990 and 1988. I added the death date of 1993 beside my mother's name. Last, I added my birthdate of 1981. I put the Bible back on the bookcase so I wouldn't pack it away unintentionally and looked at the frames stacked against the bookcase.

The first two frames held generic landscape prints. The third contained a colorful drawing of the whole estate, which looked very much like the scene I had encountered upon our arrival on Saturday evening. It was beautiful in its simplicity as if a child had drawn it. I glanced at the corner and saw it was signed Mavis Levy, 1945.

Granny Mavis had loved to paint and draw, but always landscapes—never portraits. She hadn't told me much about growing up in Bettencourt, but she had always been willing to talk about her latest painting to teach me a few techniques. I had felt like such a big kid getting to use her paints when I had been so young, though I had no talent for it at all. Mavis had never taken any formal art lessons. She had taught herself out of love for the hobby.

I had been only nine when she had died, but I could remember how sad she had been after Grandpa had died of a heart attack. She hadn't drawn or painted anymore. It was like a light had turned off inside her. She had lingered in the hospital for her last month or so in heart failure. Mom had told us Granny had died of a broken heart just like Grandpa.

After I had placed Granny's drawing to the side to save, I looked through the other frames. They all contained painted portraits of men and women in older-style clothing, seated in elegant chairs or standing near bookcases. I wished I knew which of the portraits belonged to the family members listed in the Bible, but none were labeled.

One portrait was a girl sitting sidesaddle on a beautiful black horse near a stable. Her red hair poked out of the front of her bonnet. On her face was a smile, but her dull blue eyes looked distant and sad. They were eyes I had seen before. *I am looking at Virginia Cooper,* I thought. I picked up the frame to get a closer look and almost dropped it as soon as I caught a glimpse of the painting stacked behind it.

I studied the portrait carefully. Brown eyes the same shade as my own stared back at me. It was the same young woman from the photograph Jon had found. The resemblance to my own face was undeniable as I looked at the likeness of her in color. I was certain it was Caroline Marshall. Her long blond hair looked like corn silk, just like mine. It was parted in the center and fell in large ringlets on the sides. She wore a cornflower blue dress and held a book in her lap. The pearl bracelet on her wrist reminded me of one my mother had when I was a child.

"There you are," Dad said from the hallway.

I gasped and stumbled backward into the bookcase. My reaction almost caused him to drop his coffee mug.

"Sorry, sweetheart. I didn't mean to startle you. What are you doing up here all by yourself?"

"Just getting a head start on some of this stuff," I said as I tried to catch my breath. I turned the frame against the wall and grabbed the drawing of the property to show him. "Look, Granny Mavis drew this when she was young."

Dad studied the drawing. "It's remarkable. She was a very talented lady," he said.

"I want to take it home with us."

"Of course you can."

"Thank you," I said. "And the Bible too. It has all the births and deaths of Mom's side of the family since this house was built." I showed it to him.

"Yes," he said. "She found it quite interesting that she could trace herself back so far, especially to the niece of Caroline Marshall. She meant to take it with us after Cadencia's funeral, but with chasing around the boys, we forgot and then we were surprised to find out about you not long after we got home."

"Dad, are you trying to tell me I was conceived in this house?"

He thought about it for a moment. "I guess you were," he said.

"Gross, Dad!" I said. "You were here for a funeral!"

He shrugged his shoulders. "It's not like we did it at the chapel," he said. "We were here for a month wrapping up Cadencia's affairs. Stuff happens. Stuff that can lead to babies. Remember that."

I had to get out of the conversation because it was getting far too uncomfortable. I thought about showing Dad the portraits, but I didn't feel like going into detail about what I had experienced in the house. I was worried he would make me start seeing the therapist again.

"Let's just go eat breakfast," I said.

"So how was the beach?" he asked as I followed him down the stairs.

"It was fine," I said.

He turned around and raised his eyebrows. "Your brothers said the exact same thing," he said. "You didn't get too spooked with all those silly ghost stories, did you? Are you sure everything's fine?"

I nodded. It had been fine for the most exciting night of my life so far. I wasn't comfortable talking to my dad about what had happened with Bo.

Chapter 14

Bo called right after I finished breakfast. There were only two phones in the house, one in the kitchen and one outside the living room. There was no way to speak with him privately, so I took the call in the kitchen.

"Hey," he said.

"Good morning."

"I'm looking forward to seeing you at the church service tonight."

"Me too," I said. "We drove past the church on our way in. It looked so pretty."

Silence followed. There had never been silence during our phone calls. I couldn't say much because Margo was standing behind me and Dad was walking in and out through the swinging door with dishes from the dining room. *Maybe I should have chosen the other phone*, I thought. Everyone else was already packing boxes upstairs. I was supposed to help in the kitchen.

"I hope I didn't freak you out too much last night," Bo said. "I don't want things to be weird with us, but honestly I can't stop thinking about it."

"Me neither," I said.

Our kiss had replayed in my mind during breakfast. I had caught myself smiling several times and had no idea what had been said in the conversations around me. I had nothing to compare it to, but the way Bo had kissed me had been amazing. I hoped all of the kisses in my life would feel like that.

"Is that good or bad?" Bo asked. "You're not talking as much as usual." He laughed nervously.

"I'm just hanging out in the kitchen with my dad and Margo."

"Oh," Bo said. He sounded relieved. "Mine aren't home. They went to the grocery store before it closes to get a few things for our lunch tomorrow. We're still planning to spend Christmas with your family."

"You'll have to see the tiny tree Trini and I decorated," I said.

"We have an artificial one," Bo said. "I love real trees, though, no matter how small they are."

"I think I stole your scarf."

"You can keep it. It looks much better on you."

"Oh, I wasn't planning on giving it back," I said. "Blue is my favorite color." I giggled. I was not usually the type of girl who did that.

"I see how you are," he said. "Did you sleep well? Any strange encounters?"

"Everything was fine, a few dreams, but I'm okay," I said. I wondered if Bo had dreamed about me too.

"I called my aunt this morning and told her what's been happening to you. She'll be at church tonight so you can talk to her then, okay?"

I felt like I was being watched. I turned around and saw that Margo and Dad were standing beside each other watching me talk on the phone. They continued their tasks after I glared at them.

"Sounds good," I said. "I have to go."

"Okay," he said. He sounded disappointed.

"Bye."

"Caroline…"

"What?"

"Um…nothing," he said. "I'll see you tonight."

I didn't want to hang up either. I could have talked to Bo on the phone all day because it was much less nerve-wracking than the thought of actually seeing him later. I realized I had twisted the phone cord around my arm while Bo and I were talking, so I had to untangle myself before I could hang up the receiver.

"I was hoping we'd have at least another year or two before the love bug bit you," Dad said.

I immediately blushed. Margo elbowed him in the ribs. He enjoyed teasing me even more than my brothers did.

"Dad!" I said.

"Don't be embarrassed," he said. "Bo's a good kid. I like him. His parents are good people, and I know he's been raised right. He's exactly the kind of boy I would choose for you if it were up to me."

"Mark," Margo said. "Caroline and I will finish up in here. Why don't you finish going through our room?"

"Fine," Dad said. "I'm trying to accept that you and Bo seem to like each other as more than friends, but if Bo isn't as nice as I think he is—I'll break his legs."

I covered my face with my hands until I heard him leave the room.

"Boys," Margo said as she rolled her eyes and shook her head.

I was dying to talk to another woman about what had happened. I couldn't call Becca because she was with her family in Paris for Christmas. I knew I could trust Margo since she hadn't told Dad my secret about the ghost.

I looked to make sure no one else was nearby to hear me. "Bo kissed me last night," I said softly.

"He did!" she whispered. She had a huge grin on her face. "Did that help with some of the confusion you were feeling?"

"Some," I said. "But it added some too."

"Like what?" she asked as she motioned for me to join her on the bar stools.

"We live so far away from each other," I said. I sat down beside Margo and propped my chin on my arms against the counter. "It's stupid, I don't even know what we're doing or what the kiss meant, but I already miss him. The distance was fine when we were just friends, but if we become more…"

"That's true," she said. "Distance can be an obstacle for couples even twice your age. Just remember what I said last night, what's meant to be will be. I have faith that if you and Bo are meant to be together someday, then you will be."

"But what do I do in the meantime?" I asked.

"Enjoy it," she said. "The best part of recovering from a first kiss is the anticipation of another one. You'll know soon enough if it meant as much to Bo as it did to you."

"He told me he didn't want things to be weird between us," I said. "But he also said he couldn't stop thinking about it."

"I think it means he cares about you."

"It's already weird. I feel like I'm too young for all this. I mean, good grief, I still played with dolls when I met him. I did really want to kiss him, though. And, oh my God, when he did I felt it in my toes." I was babbling. *Shut up,* I told myself.

Margo smiled. "Time passes so quickly sometimes. You'll blink, and you'll be as old as me," she said. "You're not too young for kissing, Caroline. It's fun and innocent. Now, you're definitely too young for some things, but not kissing."

I was embarrassed again. "I know!" I said. "Believe me. That's so far away."

"Oh, it's closer than you think," she said. "You can always talk to me. But I can tell already you'll make smarter decisions than I did at your age. I know it doesn't help, but try not to worry so much."

"I'll try," I said. "And Margo, I don't think you're old."

She smiled again. "Now how are you feeling otherwise?" she asked. "Since Sunday?"

"I think I'm okay. But, I do want to show you something," I said.

I had Margo follow me to the living room. I reached under the table and pulled out the photograph. When she saw it, her mouth dropped open.

"Oh my," she said. She took it from me to get a closer look. "The similarity is remarkable. Her eyes even appear dark like yours."

"I saw the ghost in the stable again yesterday afternoon. I think it's unlikely I hallucinated the same thing twice," I said. "The ghost thinks I'm Caroline Marshall and I think it's her in that photograph. I found a portrait of her upstairs too. It's just too much for all these things to be coincidences. Please don't tell Dad. I'm so afraid he'll think I'm crazy."

"Sweetie, I really think you should tell him," she said. "I know he acts silly sometimes teasing you, but I know he would want to know what's going on."

"Please don't," I begged. "I have to figure it out myself first before Dad has me committed. The little girl is Virginia Cooper who was the sister of Thomas, Caroline's beau."

It was strange using that word, her beau versus my Bo. I immediately felt foolish thinking of Bo as mine.

We had told Margo about the legend during our drive to Bettencourt. Dad had always said the deaths were true and could be proven, but all the hauntings were hogwash and mass hysteria as far as he was concerned.

"I won't tell him as long as I don't think you're in danger," she said. "So what are we going to do?"

I decided not to tell her about the encounter I had in my room because it was much more frightening than the stable. "Bo says his aunt can help me. She seems to have a connection to things like this," I said. "She'll be at church tonight. Serena is Bob's older sister."

"I'm anxious to meet her," Margo said. "I'll do whatever I can to help. Just promise you'll keep telling me what's going on."

"I will," I said. I wasn't sure if Margo was talking about things with Bo or the ghost, but I would continue to talk to her about both.

Everyone else was spread out in different rooms on the third floor. I found my brothers and had them follow me into the room above mine. They were shocked when I showed them the painting of Virginia, but even more so when I showed them the one I thought was Caroline.

"You two really were identical," Brad said as he studied it carefully. "Even your eyes are the same color."

"I found this too," I said. I placed the Bible on a desk near the window, opened it, and pointed to the writing on the inside cover. "Look at all this. I updated it this morning."

Jon read through it and then went back to Bonnie's family. "This is really strange," he said. "Everywhere else, the word 'twins' is written except for with Antoinette and Weston."

I hadn't noticed when I first read through the records, but he was right.

"Maybe she was the smaller twin, and they thought she might not make it," Brad said. "They could have waited to write her name down later."

"No," I said. "I don't think so. It's sad, but there are some baby deaths recorded in here. And one of the death dates seems like the woman died giving birth. It's probably just because different people were keeping the records then."

We shrugged it off and went back to cleaning and packing up things. As I thought of the whole house, I was overwhelmed with how much stuff was in it and we hadn't even gone into the attic yet.

That afternoon was even warmer than the day before, with temperatures several degrees above freezing. The yard was a muddy mess when we took boxes to the storage container and the dumpster behind the house. We stopped briefly to snack for lunch and then worked a few more hours.

We stopped working in the late afternoon so we would have time to get ready for our evening with Bo's family. Sharing one bathroom was getting frustrating. I had to put on my make-up by lantern light in my bedroom. I wanted to look as pretty as possible in the dress I planned to wear.

Before we left home, I had packed my mother's short-sleeved red velvet dress. She had always worn it on Christmas Eve. It was one of only a few things we had kept when we'd donated her clothing. My entire body tingled as I slipped on the soft dress and pulled up the zipper. It fit me perfectly, and the beaded embellishments along the low neckline made me look much older than fifteen. I didn't think Dad would let me out of the house dressed as I was.

I put on thick tights, my black boots, and a cardigan sweater, all of which made me look a bit less grown up. Even with the warmer temperatures during the day, the nights were still clear and cold, so I wanted to be prepared. After I had brushed my hair, I glanced in the mirror. I had hoped to look like Mom, but the reflection I saw no longer looked like me or her; it looked like Caroline Marshall.

Chapter 15

Dad came out of his room as I entered the hallway. His mouth dropped open, then he struggled with his words. I waited for him at the top of the stairs.

"Oh, Caroline, I thought I had lost my mind for a moment and traveled back in time," he said as he hugged me. "You…you look so much like your mother."

"Thank you," I said. "I hope you don't mind me wearing her dress."

"Of course not, honey, you look beautiful," he said. "Now, we may have to pick up Bo off the floor when he sees you. I know I've said no dating until you're sixteen, but for you and him I could probably make an exception."

Had Margo broken my trust?

"Did Margo tell you?" I asked.

"Tell me what?" he asked.

I studied his reaction. Either he didn't know or was doing a great job of acting like he didn't.

"Nothing," I said.

Something about being around my dad made me want to stay a little girl forever in his mind.

"I'm glad you have Margo to talk to," Dad said. "She wouldn't have to tell me anything; I can tell by looking at Bo that he's in love with you. I am getting older, but I still remember what it was like when I was his age and fell in love with your mother. I wasn't that much older than you."

"That's quite a leap, Dad," I said.

Bo in love with me, could it be possible?

"I don't think so," he said.

"How did you know you loved Mom?"

"I can't explain it," he said. "You just know. Trust me."

I was already nervous about seeing Bo again, and Dad's comments made it worse. The anticipation of a second kiss was on my mind because the first had meant something to me, but I didn't think we would get the chance with our families around. I kept reminding myself he was the same sweet, caring Bo I had known since I was eight years old.

Focusing on Bo helped keep my mind off of the uneasy feeling I had whenever I thought about everything else that had happened. Each creak or pop I heard in the house made me quickly look in its direction. Everywhere I looked, though, I found nothing unusual.

We had sandwiches again for dinner. Trini and Jack complained a little, but I didn't care. My nerves kept me from being hungry, so I mostly picked at my food. By the time we left, my hands felt clammy in my gloves.

The drive into town went by quickly. The church was a large white colonial-style building with a square bell tower at the front. A rectangular addition extended from the right side of the main building. The cemetery was on the left side, lit by the lampposts scattered throughout.

Bo was standing inside the main doors waiting for us when we arrived. We were early for the service, so we met several of Marlene and Bob's friends. Dad and Margo went with them into the sanctuary. Some kids took Jack and Trini to see the children's church area. Brad talked with Bo's friends from the beach and a few other teenagers at the front of the sanctuary. Jon and Justice sat on a pew together and traded insults. I stayed with Bo while he helped me hang my coat on the hooks in the entryway.

"I want to show you something," he said.

Bo took a key out of his pocket and opened a door in the entryway. Once we stepped inside, he pulled the door closed behind us. It took a moment for my eyes to adjust to the darkness, and then with the light from outside shining in through the windows, I saw a staircase. Bo took my hand and led me up the winding stairs until we reached a platform at the top. The floors were wide wooden planks that creaked beneath our weight. A large dark bell hung far above the thick beams that stretched across the space above us. The only light came from windows in the center of each of the four walls.

"Wow," I said as I looked around. "This is incredible."

"Come look out over here," Bo said. He was standing beside the window that faced the cemetery.

I was glad to be so close to him again. Bo stood behind me with his hand on my shoulder and pointed out the Bettencourt graves. They had the largest headstones and were in a separate area with an ornate cast-iron fence. There was a lamppost nearby that lit the graves and a couple of benches.

"It's obvious who ruled this town," he said.

"Well, it was named after them," I said.

"Way back there is where you can see the lighthouse if you come up here during the day. If there's a full moon and a clear night you can see it then too," he said.

He pointed to the darkened area far beyond the cemetery past the shore. The winding coastline formed cove area on the border of the town.

"So you've been up here a lot?" I asked.

"It's a pretty popular spot," he said.

"What?" I turned around to face him. I wondered, had he brought someone else here?

"Oh," he said. He laughed nervously. "Not for me, for other people. I work here with Mom to help clean the place. I always come up here to sweep the cobwebs and check for leaks. During the summer I found some, um, questionable trash, so we have to keep it locked now. Only those of us on the cleaning crew have keys."

"Questionable trash?"

"Yeah," he said. "According to the elders, there was some morally objectionable activity happening in here."

"In a church?" I asked. I was shocked. I had trouble imagining what some people did in parked cars; I couldn't believe people would go that far in a church.

Bo shrugged his shoulders. "I guess they got carried away," he said. "I wouldn't know…"

It made me feel better to know, that when it came to relationships, neither of us knew what we were doing.

I looked out the window again. "Thank you for bringing me here," I said. "It's beautiful."

"You are," he said. "This is just an old building with a view."

I turned back to him. He pushed his glasses up higher on his nose and smiled at me. There was that feeling Margo had told me about. Anticipation. It had taken over my mind. Bo brushed his fingers against my cheek and started to speak again, but I kissed him before he could. It was much less rushed and softer than the night before, but I still felt butterflies in my stomach.

Afterward, I rested my head on his chest and wrapped my arms around his waist. He hugged me tightly in return, his arms around my shoulders. I heard his heart pounding and felt my own doing the same. It felt like we were dancing even though I knew we were standing still.

Bo's lips brushed against the top of my head when he spoke. "I think we're in trouble," he whispered.

I closed my eyes and hugged him tighter. "I know," I said.

If he felt anything close to what I did, we really were in trouble. Everything felt new, exciting and intimidating all at the same time, but I didn't want to let go. Ever. I wasn't sure how long we stood there, but I opened my eyes when I sensed we were not alone. I had not heard Justice come up the stairs and Bo hadn't known either because he was startled when she spoke.

"Hey, Bo, they need you on the candle crew," Justice said.

"Crap," he whispered as he let go of me. He turned to Justice. "I forgot. Can you take Caroline to the seats we saved?"

"Sure," Justice said. She turned back to me when Bo was out of sight. "Bo's always been more like a brother to me than a cousin. We've grown up together."

"Yeah," I said. "Bo's talked about you a lot."

"He never shuts up about you," she said with a sigh and crossed her arms. "I wondered when I met you last night if you had any idea he's completely in love with you and has been since he was like thirteen—maybe even younger. Our entire family knows, and nearly all of his friends have figured it out, but you didn't know, did you?"

Bo loved me? Was my father right? I began to think about all of his actions from the time of my mother's death to the wedding to the kiss. Bo had never told me, but it made sense. It was more than just attraction.

"I guess I didn't," I said. "He's my best friend. I never thought of him like that until n—"

Justice interrupted me. "When he showed me your picture, and I saw how gorgeous you were with your long blond hair and dainty features, I assumed you'd be shallow," she said. "Of course, everything he told me about you contradicted that. I can see that you're not. I should have known Bo could never fall for anyone like that. I judged you based on your appearance, and I'm sorry."

I just stood there and didn't know how to respond. I wasn't sure whether to be insulted or grateful for her honesty. I had never thought of myself as particularly gorgeous. Pretty, maybe, but nowhere near as beautiful as my mother had been. But I definitely wasn't shallow.

Justice tilted her head to the side. I felt like she could read my mind.

"He told me this morning that he kissed you last night," Justice said. "That kiss—his first—meant everything to him. He's not a casual guy. Bo analyzes everything, and he was worried he might have destroyed your friendship."

"Never," I said. "That's not possible."

"I realize I don't really know you, but what I just witnessed didn't look casual for you either," she said. "You kissed him and then clung to him like you were drowning. Like someone might try to rip him away."

I was embarrassed that she'd seen what I had thought was a private moment with Bo. I bit my lip and nodded because I couldn't think of what to say.

Justice looked me in the eyes. "You know what I think?" she asked. "I think you're in love with him too and just figured it out yourself."

She's right, I thought. *Oh my God, I'm in love with* Bo. It was like what Dad had said; I just knew. I felt tears welling up in my eyes. My feelings for him had grown in the background, and I hadn't noticed because I had been so self-absorbed. I had no idea how I was going to say goodbye to him when I had to go home and then not see him again for who knows how long. The way Justice looked at me told me I had confirmed her observation without speaking.

"Look, I know you're young, but time has a way of taking care of that. I'm not trying to be bitchy, just please don't break his heart," she said as she motioned for us to go down the stairs. "He'd die before breaking yours. There aren't many people like that out there anymore."

Justice was different than anyone else I had ever met. She came across as confrontational and rude, but she had a lot of valid things to say and was willing to admit when she was wrong. I could tell she had a good heart, and I wanted to be her friend. She was only eighteen, but to me, she seemed to possess the wisdom of a person much older.

"Jon's like that too, you know," I said as we reached the halfway point on the stairs.

"He's cute, but we don't get along," she said.

I laughed. "He said the same thing about you," I said.

"Great minds…" she said with a shrug and shared in my laughter.

"Can you and your mom really help me?" I asked as we stood outside the sanctuary.

I felt like she could see right through me when she looked at me. Her eyes were the same blue as Bo's but seemed brighter because of her black hair.

"I hope so," she said as she placed her hand on my shoulder.

Chapter 16

My family was already seated in the back two pews when Justice and I walked in the sanctuary. Justice watched as I sat beside Jon and then she went to the next pew and sat beside a dark-haired woman I assumed was her mother, who was sitting next to Bob. Marlene, Dad, and Margo were sitting there too. Jack and Trini were on the other side of Brad. They had left a space for Bo and me.

Bo was at the front with a few other teenagers getting the candles ready for the service. He smiled at me when he handed me a candle. The lights were dimmed and the choir sang several songs, including "Hark! The Herald Angels Sing," which had been Mom's favorite. After the singing, we blew out our candles, and the lights were brought back up again so we could see the pastor.

I didn't pay attention to the sermon as much as I should have. Bo's hand was on top of mine, and all I could think about was what Justice had said about Bo being in love with me. Everyone else had known before I had—Bo's friends and family, my family, Becca. Even Justice had realized I was in love with Bo right before I had. How could I have been the last to know?

A small dessert reception started in the fellowship hall after the service. Bo whispered that we should slip away to see the cemetery. He tapped Justice on the shoulder and told her about our plans during all the noise as people prepared to leave the sanctuary.

Justice said she would bring her mother to meet us as soon as possible. We managed to get away without anyone noticing since everyone else was heading in the opposite direction. After we put on our coats, Bo took me out a side door and led me to the cemetery gates. He took me to the Bettencourt graves first.

While I was walking near the fence, I accidentally stepped on the corner of a grave and immediately felt chilled. I knelt beside it and placed my hand in the center where the snow had melted away. I was certain the grave belonged to Caroline Marshall. Bo and I looked at the stone. It was smooth with age, and we couldn't read a name on it.

"This is Caroline's grave," I said. I started to feel a bit nauseated and lightheaded.

"How do you know?" Bo asked.

"I'm not sure," I said. "I just feel it."

I was suddenly overcome with an intense and overwhelming sense of loss. It took my breath away so I had to sit down on the bench. I could tell Bo was worried about me.

"Are you okay?" he asked. He sat down beside me and placed his hand on my cheek.

I tried to catch my breath and not cry, but I couldn't stop the tears from streaming down my cheeks while I processed everything. Bo wrapped his arms around me and held me until I was able to stop crying. His touch was so comforting that I felt calmer within a few minutes.

"I'm sorry," I said. "I'm a mess. All I do is cry lately. You should probably reconsider hanging out with me."

"Never," he said as he looked behind us. "My aunt and Justy are coming. Do you still want to talk to them?"

"I have to," I said. I dried my face with a tissue I found in my coat pocket and wiped off most of my make-up in the process. I still felt tightness in my chest and a lump in my throat. It felt like impending doom.

Bo held my hand. "Everything will be okay," he said. "I know they can help."

The pretty dark-haired woman I had seen earlier, who looked like a slightly older version of Justice, approached us. Bo introduced me to her.

"You can call me Serena," she said as she extended her hand for me to shake. "Bo tells me you need my help."

"Yes ma'am," I said as I took her hand. "I hope I'm not wasting your time."

Serena held my hand between both of her hands before she let go. "I am willing to help you with anything I can, dear. Anything for Roberta's daughter," she said.

"How well did you know my mother?" I asked.

"Very well," Serena said. "We were good friends. Did she ever tell you about the séance?"

"She told us a lot, but she never mentioned a séance," I said. "She wrote about it in a diary I found, but she wrote that nothing happened."

"That's not true. Something happened that night. I re-member like it was yesterday," Serena said.

She and Justice sat on the bench. Bo and I stood in front of them, facing the church. I saw my brothers walking toward us.

"Wait just a minute, my brothers will want to hear this," I said. I motioned for them to come over to us.

Jon and Brad walked over quickly. Brad stood beside me, and Jon sat down beside Justice.

"Serena was about to tell us about the séance," I said to my brothers.

"Great," Brad said.

"We decided to hold a séance the night of the Fourth of July party," Serena said. "It had been cloudy all day so we weren't surprised when the rain started and we were all forced inside. Six of us went upstairs to Roberta's room: her, me, Marlene, Bob, Gary—who is Wesley's father, and my ex-husband James. We lit candles and sat in a circle in front of the fireplace. The storm outside was growing more intense, but we were young and feared nothing. We thought we were invincible."

"Mom and Dad were there?" Bo asked. "They never told me about that."

"Yes," Serena said. "Contacting the spirit of Caroline Marshall was our priority. We began to chant for her spirit, almost yelling over the sound of the wind, rain, and thunder. Because we were in a circle, we all noticed at the same time when Roberta's eyes became so glassy they seemed to be glowing in the candlelight.

"She spoke to us, but it was in a bittersweet voice lacking Roberta's accent, and said plain as day 'She's not here yet.' There was a huge clap of thunder and a flash of lightning. All the candles went out, and we heard screams from downstairs because the power had gone out at that exact moment."

"What does that mean?" Brad asked. "Who wasn't there yet?"

"The right person to help the spirit," Justice said. "It has to be someone strong enough to understand."

I could tell Jon was nervous because he kept kicking the gravel under the bench.

"We were so frightened," Serena said. "Roberta had no memory of what happened; it was like she had blacked out. Every fuse had blown because lightning struck the house. I'll never forget that night. I haven't ever encountered another spirit presence that left me feeling as sad as the ones at Bettencourt Estate. There is a lot of heartache trapped there."

Heartache was exactly what I felt. I could sense Caroline's pain mixing with my own.

"But what does all that mean for our Caroline?" Brad asked. "Did she tell you what's been happening?"

"Bo told me," Serena said. "Has anything else happened?"

"We found a painting and a photo of a young woman who looks exactly like me," I said. "The photo's dated 1846. I think it's Caroline."

"Ah, a namesake lookalike and kindred spirit," Justice said as she raised her arms to the sky. "It all makes sense now."

Jon stared at her and then shook his head.

"Of course," Serena said. "The spirits needed someone to connect with who truly understands great sorrow. That's you, Caroline, because of your mother."

"But what am I supposed to do?" I asked. I was desperate for answers.

"Don't be afraid of them," Serena said. "You just have to find out what they want. If you can help them, they'll be able to move on. When I was in the house I never felt like the spirits there were harmful."

"How do I do that?" I asked.

"Ask them," Serena said. "Find out what they want and help them understand it's time to move on. That's what I try to do for other families who need my services."

"Services?" Jon asked as he raised his eyebrows and looked at Justice. His skepticism was returning.

Justice scoffed and turned away from him.

"Psychic medium services, palm-reading, haunting consultations," Serena said. "I began feeling spirit connections when I was quite young—eleven or twelve."

"Yeah, me too," Justice said. "I knew when I shook your hand, Caroline, that something was troubling you—a spirit trying to connect with you."

Serena stood and walked over to me. "May I?" she asked.

She took off her gloves, and I removed mine so she could feel my hands. She closed her eyes for a moment and then let go. It was so dark where I was standing I could barely see her eyes when she looked at me.

"See what I mean, Mom?" Justice asked. She went to the same grave I thought belonged to Caroline, looked down at it and sighed.

"New love," Serena said. She glanced at Bo, then back at me. "Old love, sadness, and fear live inside you, but I'm certain you have the strength to handle this. Open your mind, free it from your resistance."

My resistance? Of course I had resisted because I'd thought I was going crazy.

"If you find you cannot handle this on your own, I'll come to the house to help you," Serena said.

She and Justice had to leave, but the rest of us stayed behind and looked at a few of the other graves. I found several of the names I remembered from the Bible records. The saddest ones were the small and simple carved headstones for everyone who had died in 1910. The names and death dates were still readable.

We left when the wind picked up, and the air started getting colder. Bo's scarf and my heaviest coat were not enough to keep me warm, but I thought it was for more reasons than just the chill in the air.

Chapter 17

Christmas Day, 1996

Trini woke us up at the crack of dawn to open presents. I could have slept all day because when I woke up, I still felt exhausted. I'd had another night of restless sleep filled with strange dreams that involved dark tunnels and spiral staircases. My legs ached like I had climbed more stairs than just the ones at the church the night before.

Margo and Dad had presents for each of us under the tree. Trini was so excited that Santa had found her. The rest of us still played along for her sake. She was as thrilled with her doll and accessories as Jack was with his personal CD player and CDs. Jon and Brad received shaving kits.

My brothers and I had chipped in to give Jack and Trini something as well but had agreed not to exchange gifts between us three until we had returned home. Dad and Margo had requested that none of us give them anything either until then.

I cried in front of everyone when I opened a small box from Dad. It was my mother's pearl bracelet. I had loved it for as long as I could remember. Mom had let me try it on many times when I was a little girl. She had promised to give it to me someday when I was old enough.

"I know you'll take very good care of it," Dad said. "It was very special to your mother. Mavis gave it to her on our wedding day."

"That's so sweet," Margo said as she came over to look at it. "This looks like an antique."

"Yes," Dad said. "Family heirloom I think. I took it to a jeweler and had it restrung to make sure it won't break on you."

I got up to hug him. "Thank you, Daddy," I said. "I love it."

After we had cleaned up the wrapping, I went back to my room. I stretched out on the bed to rest for just a moment, but I fell asleep. Even while napping, my dreams were disturbing. I dreamed I was trapped in a dark tunnel with a sloping brick floor. I woke up suddenly after I experienced the sensation of falling. I was facing the outside wall of my room and could see the lighthouse through the window. There was a strong hand on my shoulder. I was relieved to see Bo sitting on the side of my bed when I turned over.

"Hey," he said. "I was trying to wake you. You were dreaming."

I sat up and hugged him. "I can't sleep at all without having nightmares," I said. "I keep dreaming about falling or being trapped in a dark place."

Bo stayed close to me. "It'll be okay," he said as he brushed my hair out of my face. He looked like he wanted to kiss me.

Dad stuck his head in from the hallway and opened the door all the way. "This door stays open," he said.

Bo jumped. "Of course, sir," he said. He moved away from me to the end of the bed.

"Lunch is about a half-hour out," Dad said as he left the room.

"A half-hour? What time is it?" I asked. It had been early morning when I got into bed. I felt disoriented.

Bo glanced at his watch. "Almost noon," he said. He got up and looked at the trunk. "My mom has one just like this."

"It has stuff in it I think belonged to Caroline," I said. "You want to see? The key is in that top desk drawer."

Bo got the key and opened the trunk. We looked through the contents together. He was careful with the delicate items but wasn't as impressed as I was with the fine sewing details on the quilt and clothing.

He noticed the rag-doll. "This makes me think of that doll you used to carry around when we were kids," he said as he put it on the floor.

"Yeah, I still have that old thing in the top of my closet."

"This trunk isn't as deep as I thought it would be," he said as we put the items back into the trunk. "Mom's trunk seems to go on forever."

"The whole thing is strange," I said. "It was locked. I found the key behind that lantern beside the bookcase. It's been sitting there undisturbed all this time."

"All these old houses have secrets," Bo said. "I've worked on some with my dad that have secret passages."

"That's really cool," I said. "Come on, I want to show you the painting." I stood up and took Bo's hand to help him off the floor.

Bo didn't let go of my hand until we got upstairs to the room above mine. I took the painting near the window so Bo could see it better.

"Oh my God," Bo said.

"I know, isn't it creepy?"

As we studied it, I noticed something familiar about the pearl bracelet on her wrist. The unique clasp was identical to the one on my bracelet.

"Bo, look," I said. I held out my wrist in front of the painting. "Dad gave me this. It was my mother's, a gift from Granny Mavis."

He took my hand and examined the bracelet. "The clasp looks the same," he said. "And I would swear this was you in a costume. This is really getting weird."

"I know, it's crazy," I said as I put down the painting. I picked up the one with the horse next and showed Bo. "This is the little girl, Virginia, the one I saw in the stable."

"There's something about her," Bo said.

I wondered if he saw what I did.

Bo studied the portrait. "Her eyes look sad," he said.

"I thought the same thing," I said. "I'll try to talk to her again to see if I can figure out what she wants like Serena said. Maybe I can get her to move on."

"Do you think she's the same spirit that's been in your room?" Bo asked.

"No," I said. "I think it's Caroline trying to communicate with me, but I don't know what she wants either. What I feel is all jumbled, it's like heartache and dread and longing. It's hard to describe."

"I think you explained it really well," Bo said. "I can understand longing."

"Yeah…"

Bo leaned against the window frame and took my hand. I felt drawn to him. When I was only a few inches away, he put his other arm around my waist and pulled me even closer.

Our lips had almost touched when I heard Dad call from downstairs that lunch was ready. We both laughed about my dad's awesome timing and then Bo kissed my forehead, which made me feel like I was melting.

When I went to the kitchen, Margo was frantically searching for the pie she had baked and left on the windowsill to cool. She looked frazzled with flour on her cheek and her hair in a messy bun. She was convinced Jack was playing a trick on her specifically because he had heard the missing pie story during our drive to Bettencourt.

"Well, if you cooked like I do, nobody would care that the pie's gone," I said.

Margo laughed. "It was a frozen pie!" she said. "I didn't take the time to make one this year."

"Don't worry, I won't tell a soul," I said. "And since the pie is gone, we don't have to."

Bo spoke from the doorway. "Did you burn the pie?" he asked. "It's okay. My mom brought sugar cookies. They're awesome."

Margo stopped looking and handed us things to take to the dining room. Dad had found the leaf for the table, so he added it and brought in extra chairs from the kitchen so all ten of us could sit together. I sat across from Bo, who smiled at me every time our eyes met.

Before we ate, Dad thanked God for letting us be together on Christmas. He also asked that Mom and Steven be able to see that their children were well. Silently, I asked for strength and courage to help the spirits in the house move on. Dad closed the blessing with the same words he always used. He asked for God to be with all those less fortunate than us.

The meal was excellent. Marlene had brought turkey and dressing, and Margo had cooked a ham and the other side dishes. Bo and I tried to help in the kitchen after we had eaten, but the ladies insisted we go away because they had it under control. Jon and Brad cleared the table and took out the trash.

Bo and I went to get more wood for the fireplaces. I felt a lot less frightened going to the stable with Bo. Bob and Dad were outside with the kids working on the antenna so they could get television reception. As we walked past them, Dad called out to us.

"That door stays open too!" he said.

"Of course, sir!" Bo said.

Bob chuckled. "Yeah, I remember those days," he said.

Bo pulled open the main stable door as far as it would go. Light filled the front of the stable, but the back was still dark without the side windows open.

"She was right there when I saw her," I said as I pointed to the stall. "Both times."

"Do you see anything now?" he asked.

"No," I said, feeling both relieved and disappointed.

"Good," Bo said as he grabbed an armload of wood. "Maybe she's moved on already."

I still felt uneasy. "No, I don't think so," I said. "She's here, just not showing herself."

"No ghost?" Brad asked as he and Jon came in. "We came to help with the wood. We used almost all of it last night."

"Not yet," I said.

We heard Bob calling for Bo to help him with the antenna.

"They need someone not so heavy to climb on the porch roof," Jon said as Bo left.

When Bo was out of sight, I felt a familiar chill throughout my body as the ghost of Virginia Cooper appeared in the stall in front of me.

"There she is!" I whispered through gritted teeth. "Look!"

"Where?" my brothers asked in unison. They both looked around.

A lump rose in my throat. "You don't see her?" I asked. I thought maybe I had lost my mind. "She's standing right there."

Brad walked to where I was pointing and immediately jumped back. "I feel something here," he said to Jon, who was looking at me.

"Virginia?" I coaxed, desperate for her to prove her existence to them. "Will you please speak to me?"

"Who are these men with you?" she asked.

Jon gasped and backed up against the woodpile. He stumbled on some loose logs at the bottom and fell backward against the pile. On his face was the look of fear, a feeling I had grown accustomed to since my arrival at Bettencourt. Brad stood in the same spot and looked bewildered.

I looked at Jon. "You hear her," I said before I turned back to Virginia. "These men are my brothers. Jon is on the woodpile and Brad is standing beside you."

"You have no brothers, Caroline," Virginia said. "Only one sister."

"My name is Caroline Douglas. I am not who you think I am," I said. "She died a long time ago. So did you."

She held her hands out in front of her and looked at them as if she were in great pain. She seemed to remember. "The fire...I was not allowed to play with the lantern," she said. "They tried to help me. I tried to save Midnight."

I covered my mouth with my hands. The horse! Midnight must have been that beautiful animal in the painting. The poor little girl had lost her parents, her brother, and Caroline. She had accidentally killed herself, her horse, and the Marshalls.

I removed my hands from my mouth so I could speak. "Was Midnight your horse?" I asked.

Whatever realization she had before seemed lost.

"You are much altered," she said. "Thomas is waiting."

"Where is he?" I asked.

"In the boathouse as you planned," she said to me. "You must go to him."

"I will go to him, I promise," I said, "But you have to move on. You shouldn't be here. It's time for you to go. Go to your parents."

She vanished before I could say anything else. I sighed with relief. The uneasiness I had felt before was gone.

"She's gone, right?" Brad asked. "I swear I think I felt her leave."

I nodded.

"What's going on?" Bo asked from behind us, which made Brad and me jump.

"She was here," I said. "But she's gone now."

"When you came in…" Brad said as he looked at Bo. "She disappeared."

The same thing had happened before when Jack had come into the stable, but this time, it felt different.

"No," I said. "I think she's actually moved on this time. I don't feel her here anymore."

Jon was pale when he got up and walked out of the stable without saying a word. As I watched him leave, I noticed something shiny sticking out from under the hay. On closer inspection, I realized it was a metal pie pan.

"It's Margo's pie pan," I said. "Remember, the pie story?"

"Of course," Brad said as he smiled. "I think all the pies are safe now."

"This is all starting to make sense," I said. I was talking to myself more than to the others.

"I'm glad you think so because I'm still confused about why I couldn't hear the ghost, but Jon could," Brad said. "What did she say?"

"I have to meet Thomas in the boathouse," I said. "We made plans."

"Caroline, are you okay?" Bo asked. He had his hands on my shoulders.

"I'm fine," I said. I suddenly felt uncomfortable again. I felt like Bo had asked me that question more than once.

"I bet it was Thomas I felt watching me in the boat-house," Brad said. "I don't think I told you about that, did I?"

"Let's go to the boathouse and find out," I said.

"What about Jon?" Bo asked.

"He'll be fine," Brad said. "He needs time. He's spent his whole life not believing. Now he can't deny it anymore. We should leave him alone."

Chapter 18

As soon as we started downhill to the boathouse, I realized how tall the lighthouse truly was. The warmer temperatures from the past few days were over, and there was a bitter chill in the air. While there was no more snow falling, what had melted was refrozen in patches of muddy ice everywhere. We chose our steps carefully to avoid slipping. Bo helped me since he was steadier on his feet.

Even with my heavy coat, a hat, and Bo's scarf, I was still shivering. Some of it was due to my nerves rather than the cold. I noticed the temperature did not seem to affect the guys.

The door would not budge when we tried to open it, but the doorknob would turn. We determined it was frozen shut. A thin layer of ice prevented us from seeing inside the windows as well.

"Look at this," Brad said. "I've never seen a door frozen shut like this. Have you?"

"A car door," I said. "But never the door to a building."

"It happens all the time," Bo said. "The melting snow on the roof from the past couple of days probably did this."

"It must have," I said as I ran my gloved fingers over the ice.

"We can check the other door. Stay here, Caroline. The dock is iced over too," Brad said.

"Be careful," I said.

My curiosity soon got the better of me. I managed to scrape a small amount of ice off the window with a flat rock that was nearby. I cupped my hands around my face and peeked inside. The light from the other side of the building shined through the windows. I could see several hooks hanging from the walls and ceiling. I noticed boxes stacked against the far wall.

As I looked around, the hair on the back of my neck stood up. On the floor, a trail of dark puddles and streaks appeared. As I followed the trail with my eyes, I discovered it led to the body of a man with severely mangled legs. His torn clothing was old fashioned—like what I had seen on Virginia. Last, I looked at his face. His dark hair and strong features were familiar to me. I had seen him before in my dreams. I knew it was Thomas.

With the shock of what I had just seen, I had to look away from the window. I quickly looked back, but there was no man and not a trace of the blood. I jumped back.

"What the hell?" I asked myself as I looked in the window again. I still saw nothing out of the ordinary. I was extremely confused and frightened. When I felt someone's hand on my shoulder, I screamed and quickly turned around.

Relieved to see it was only Bo, I threw my arms around his neck. "It's you!" I said. "You scared me to death!"

Bo hugged me back. "I scared you? You scared me!" he said.

Brad walked up to us. "What's going on?" he asked. He pointed to my peephole. "Is there something in there? Did you see him?"

I pulled away from Bo. "I can't go in there," I said as I tried not to hyperventilate. "It was too awful, his legs, his body. There was so much blood."

"Hey, hey," Bo said as he pulled me back into his arms. "It's okay. You don't have to go in there."

"Nobody's going in there right now," Brad said. "The windows are all locked from the inside, and the other door is locked with a padlock that's rusted shut. We'll have to come back and pry this door open or cut the other lock with bolt cutters."

"If we're right about me looking like Caroline, it will cause more problems if Thomas sees me," I said. "It has to be Jon."

"I'll go talk to him," Brad said. He pointed to his bedroom window where Jon was standing and looking out at us. "He's watching us anyway."

Bo and I walked to the base of the lighthouse, carefully avoiding the ice. We looked at the corroded lock Bob had mentioned. I stood back and admired the mysterious structure. I leaned against the rough brick wall, which snagged my gloves as I ran my fingers across it. I experienced so many powerful memories that were not my own—they were hers—the same images haunting my dreams. I saw Thomas' beautiful blue eyes, his smile, and felt the warmth of his embrace. I felt incredible sadness for my relative who should have been able to live her life with the man she loved.

"I just don't understand," I said. "Why did I see him in the boathouse if he died jumping off the lighthouse?"

"I don't know," Bo said. "I guess it's possible he survived the fall and crawled there. We'll figure it out. Justy can probably let us in the library tomorrow to see if we can find anything in the newspapers."

"Okay," I said.

I glanced back at the house. I felt calmer being farther away from the boathouse. Jon wasn't standing by the window anymore. Bo looked at me, but I wasn't sure if what I saw on his face was pity or concern. I wanted to kiss him again and forget about everything else.

"What are you thinking about?" he asked.

"I'm just wondering if I'm strong enough to help her spirit," I said.

"You are. You're the strongest person I know."

"You can't be serious. I'm terrified, and I cry all the time. Seriously, all the time."

"Crying or being afraid doesn't make you weak," Bo said. "You're amazing. You always have been. With everything you've been through with your mom…I don't think I could handle that even half as well as you have and you're still standing. And you still smile and laugh."

Crap. I couldn't stop my tears. Bo wiped my cheeks with the back of his glove then wrapped his arms around me and kissed me on the forehead for the second time that day.

Okay, I thought, *I might actually die if I don't kiss him again soon.*

I sat down on a large rock. Bo stood beside me and leaned against the base of the lighthouse.

"It sounds weird, but even with everything that's happened, I don't want to leave this place," I said. "I feel so much more at home here than I ever have back in Dardanelle. And closer to my mom."

"I wish you lived here," Bo said. He looked out at the ocean. "I don't know what it's like to not feel at home. I love living here by the ocean. I could stay here my whole life."

"I wish I lived here too."

He sat down beside me. "Do you still want to teach history someday?"

I was surprised he remembered. I hadn't really talked much about teaching since I was a kid and fell in love with history. "Yeah," I said. "I think so."

"So two and a half more years of school for you, plus four years of college," Bo said. "I'll have a year less than you."

"Then what?" I asked. "Do you still want to work with your dad?"

"Yeah, but college first like he did so when I do take over I'll know how to run it," Bo said. "There's a program here that mixes the business classes with hands-on training. I'm glad I still have a little more time to think about it, though."

"Yeah, my brothers seem so ready for what's next. Jon has a scholarship lined up, and Brad has the Navy. I just have to try to get through geometry without stabbing the guy behind me with my compass."

Bo laughed. "That same jerk is still bothering you?" he asked.

"Yes," I said. "It's fine. It'll be over soon enough." I shivered.

"Are you getting too cold?" Bo asked. He put his arm around me. "We can go back inside."

"Can we please stay here a little while longer?" I asked. "I want to talk to you."

"Sure," he said. "Anything you want."

I was freezing, but I didn't want to go back inside. I wanted to talk to Bo about more than just my geometry class and plans for college. I pushed everything else out of my mind and decided it was time because I had no idea how many more opportunities we would have to be alone. I had to know where we stood. I already knew he loved me and had realized I loved him too, but I needed to hear him say it.

"What did you mean last night when you said you think we're in trouble?" I asked.

"I thought you knew," he said.

"Everything in my head is so mixed up right now. What are we doing?"

It felt like hours passed before he spoke again.

"I thought I could live the rest of my life with you as my best friend and just be okay," he said. "I didn't think anyone as amazing as you could ever think of me as more than a friend."

"Bo…" I said. I thought he was amazing, not me.

"When you were upset at the beach, the whole time I just kept thinking that I wanted to kiss you," he said. "I was selfish."

I had wanted to kiss him the entire time we were at the beach, too. I was glad it hadn't been just me who had thought that way. I wanted to kiss him again right then too but figured I shouldn't interrupt him. The wind started blowing against my back.

Bo brushed my hair out of my face. "I know," he said. "I'm terrible."

"No, you're not," I said. "You're the least selfish person I know. I couldn't have gotten through Mom's death or the last three years without you. I remember you holding my hand at her funeral. It helped me so much." I took Bo's hand and squeezed it.

"Last night I wanted to tell you, but you kissed me before I could get past my nerves," he said. "I think—I hope you meant it and it wasn't just because I told you you're beautiful. If you feel...there's so much with our ages and the distance."

"It wasn't just a reaction," I said as I gently touched his cheek with my other hand.

He sighed and looked up at the sky for a moment, then closed his eyes.

"Bo, what is it?" I asked.

"Caroline, I—I can't remember a time when I wasn't in love with you," Bo said quickly. He looked terrified when his eyes met mine again.

I couldn't help but smile at him. It didn't matter that we were too young or that we lived twelve hundred miles away from each other. It didn't matter that having a relationship with him wasn't practical. I didn't care that I was in the middle of the most frightening time of my life; all I wanted was to be with him.

I took a deep breath and shared another first with him. "Bo," I said. "I love you too."

"As more than a friend?" he asked. He looked both cautious and hopeful. "Really?"

"We're definitely more than friends," I said.

I had never seen such a huge smile on his face. He grabbed ahold of me and kissed me with such intensity I felt like the biggest dream of my life had just come true—a dream I didn't even know I had until a couple of days ago.

"We'll find a way to be together," Bo said when we finally came up for air. His forehead was touching mine. "I'll come see you during spring break, and then maybe you can come here during the summer. If you want to. We can see how it goes, right?"

"We will," I said. I was short of breath but kissed him again anyway. "We'll figure it out, but right now we have to go back inside. I can't feel my nose."

Bo laughed. "Me neither," he said. "Come on."

He took my hand to help me off the rock, and we walked back to the house still holding hands. I thought I saw someone in the living room window, but there was no one there when I looked again.

When we got back inside, Margo and Marlene were in the dining room talking, and Dad and Bob were watching sports with the kids in the living room. We hung our coats and started upstairs, thinking we had gone unnoticed.

Halfway up the stairs, I heard my dad.

"The door stays open!" he said.

"Yes, sir!" Bo said. Then he whispered to me. "How does he do that?"

I shrugged. I had no idea.

We went to my room, left the door wide open as my father had instructed, and sat on my bed. Bo handed me a small white box he had pulled from his pocket.

"I want you to have this," he said.

I opened the box and found inside an antique silver cross necklace with three tiny clear stones mounted on it.

"It belonged to my grandmother, Mom's mother," he said. "Mom gave it to me a long time ago and said it would protect me and to give it to someone special someday. I want it to protect you."

"It's beautiful, Bo. Thank you so much," I said.

Bo helped me fasten it around my neck. I glanced down at it and then hugged him.

"I feel safer already," I said.

I noticed the rag-doll was still out on the floor beside the trunk. As I began to put it away, I had a random memory about the bottom of the trunk coming apart. Instead of putting the doll back, I started taking everything out again.

"What are you doing?" Bo asked.

"There's something else in here," I said. "I think it has a false bottom."

I put my fingers in the holes at the bottom and lifted out the wooden planks. A small brown leather-bound book was resting on the real bottom of the trunk.

As soon as I picked it up, I knew what it was. I carefully opened the book to reveal the elegant cursive writing inside. It was a diary; the pages had yellowed with age. The first entry was on Christmas Day, 1845.

"Oh my God, Bo," I said. "This is Caroline Marshall's diary."

We sat on the floor with our backs against the bed and flipped through the pages to learn as much as we could about her. Jack and Trini came up once each at separate times while we were reading. They looked at me, waved, and then returned downstairs. I assumed they were spying for my dad to make sure the door was still open.

Chapter 19

Caroline Marshall's Diary

25 December 1845

As this season of joy is in progress, memories of Grandmother Elberta sadden me. If she were still alive, I feel my engagement plans would be less perplexed. Mother and Father insist that I marry Sebastian Collierman III. The wedding is scheduled for late July 1847, shortly after I am eighteen. I desire marriage for love to someone who is not twelve years older. I long to become Mrs. Thomas Cooper.

He feels we were brought together by fate, as were Romeo and Juliet. I fear we might be fated to their tragic end, as we too find ourselves separated by society.

27 December 1845

I awoke from a horrific dream this morning. I dreamed of death, my own. Perhaps I feel regret for misleading my mother and father? I have no intention of marrying Sebastian. I will run away with Thomas before the wedding date. Thomas is concerned they will no longer care for Virginia if he is gone. I told him she could come with us.

15 January 1846

My tutor arrives at eight o'clock and leaves at eleven o'clock, leaving my afternoons unoccupied. I spend time with Thomas in the lighthouse every day. With me, I take the works of Shakespeare for us to discuss. His favorite is Romeo and Juliet. I must disagree with my love, for I feel Hamlet or Macbeth are far more interesting. We quarreled about this difference of opinion, but Thomas would never speak ill to me.

Although Sebastian is intelligent and handsome, I do not love him. Mother believes that love follows marriage, but I feel love should come first. Bonnie was fortunate to be in love with the man to whom she was engaged. If only I could be as fortunate.

I desire to grow old with Thomas, to be his wife and bear his children. I wish I did not have to run away to be with him. I am fortunate my father insists I wait until age eighteen to marry.

7 February 1846

The most terrible of events has occurred tonight. My family held a ball in honor of my engagement and wedding, which has been moved to this summer. Father now feels seventeen is old enough to be married. One day arranged marriages will come to an end, I hope.

Sebastian is a delightful man. He is so kind to me, but I do not love him as I love Thomas. I prayed for an engagement as long as that of my sister so some acts of fate could prevent our union. If only I could encounter a band of witches to warn me of future events as in Macbeth. The best witches' warning: "Caroline, fear not the wrath of your father, but the wrath of not obeying your heart."

27 February 1846

My day began so dreadfully; I thought nothing could make it pleasant. I was forced by Mother to sit for hours while an artist painted my portrait. I prefer sitting only minutes for a photograph, though Mother feels a portrait is more lifelike. I must admit she is correct. The artist mixed his paints perfectly to depict my favorite light blue dress. He included the pearl bracelet on my wrist that was a gift from Grandmother Elberta.

23 March 1846

Today I stood for hours in my undergarments while a visiting tailor took measurements for my wedding gown. It will be lovely, but I wish I were having it made for a wedding with Thomas.

Tonight I went to him and cried about the beautiful wedding gown. Thomas brushed the tears off my cheeks. Soon we were kissing and then I was in my undergarments for the second time today. I am not certain why we were unable to stop as we have before. We have sinned.

My wedding will not take place; for Thomas has assured me he is saving money for us to run away soon. He says we will leave Bettencourt and not let it happen again until we are married. I have prayed for God's forgiveness for our sin of expressing love before marriage. Mother and Father would disown me if they knew.

11 May 1846

A ball was held tonight in honor of Father's birthday. I have spent the evening lying down because of an incident at the ball. I did not feel well this morning, but I could not miss the celebration. As Sebastian and I were dancing, I suddenly felt odd. He was helping me to a chair when I fainted before a room full of Father's friends. Sebastian carried me to my bed and told me what had happened when I stirred.

I wish to never show my face at a ball again. It would be embarrassing if anyone spoke of my having fainted at my father's celebration. After Sebastian had left me to rest, Thomas came to my bedside. He needs more money before he will have enough for a horse and carriage to take us away.

18 May 1846

Bonnie and Weston arrived this morning. They were unable to get here in time for the ball because they were packing their belongings. Wes-

ton is needed here so they will stay with us until they can find a suitable house. Bonnie is expecting a child at the end of December or early January.

I am sad I will not be here to meet my niece or nephew. Bonnie hopes her baby is a boy. In fact, she told me she already knows the child she carries is a boy. Of course Bonnie wants a daughter someday, but she feels it is best for the boy to be first so he can protect his sister. It is wonderful to have my sister back in the room next to mine.

30 May 1846

Bonnie and I had a long talk in the ballroom as we did years ago when we visited our grandparents. It is wonderful living in this house.

Grandmother Elberta told me secrets about this house that even Mother does not know. I miss her so. Thomas is the only person who knows what she told me about the passage.

My sister confided in me the symptoms of her condition: feeling ill in the mornings, feeling faint in the evenings, craving salt and most of all, feeling irritable about things that should be insignificant. Mother feels it is not proper for women to discuss the condition of pregnancy, but Bonnie does not agree.

As Bonnie spoke of her complaints, I realized I have much to fear. I am not certain, but I might be carrying a child as well. I have experienced many things Bonnie described. I have not had a monthly since I was with Thomas. What will become of me? What becomes of unwed mothers? How shall I tell Thomas? I have forgotten Sebastian. This could prevent my wedding because he will be ashamed of me, but I cannot tell because Mother and Father will be disgraced. I did not tell Bonnie. I must first wait to see if my suspicions were formed too quickly.

19 June 1846

I am now certain my initial suspicions were correct. I am pregnant. I had to loosen my corset with my sewing scissors, and I fear my garments will no longer fit in a few weeks. This child is truly a blessing, as is Bonnie's child. It is a pity I shall have to hide my condition for as long as possible until I decide what actions to follow. I know I must tell Thomas soon. He will suggest we run away to get married, but I am in no condition to travel. I feel so very ill when I wake in the mornings. There must be something I can do. God, please help me in my journey. Please do not punish the child inside me for my sins.

21 June 1846

I have confided in my sister, who sobbed with me as I told her. The burden of my secret still lies heavy in my thoughts because I have yet to tell another soul. Now that I have told Bonnie, I feel the baby exists. Until now, there was always the possibility I was mistaken or asleep in a nightmare.

Bonnie pulled out a chart and helped me count back. We have determined that my child should be born before hers, in the middle of December.

My wedding day of 25 July is growing nearer, which means my secret must be revealed soon. I continue to pray for a way to escape the shame my family will face. If only my impending marriage were delayed, I might have another month to decide how to tell Mother and Father. With help from Bonnie, I believe I can conceal my condition for at least one more month. How I wish Grandmother Elberta were alive. She would help me.

1 July 1846

    God has answered my prayers. Sebastian's father has fallen ill. I received a note from a messenger this morning that Sebastian had requested we postpone the wedding until next summer when we originally intended to marry. Sebastian is traveling to see his father. I do feel bad for Mr. Collierman, but it must be God's will.

20 July 1846

    My family hosted a dinner in my honor today for my seventeenth birthday. They believe I am sad about my wedding postponement.

    I went to Thomas this evening and told him my secret. For the longest while, he said nothing. I spoke to him, asking him questions, but he would not answer. Finally, he smiled and told me how happy he was to hear my news. He wants to run away at the end of next month, but I fear I shouldn't travel.

29 August 1846

    Even with my sister's help, I can no longer hide my condition. Mother came into my room while Bonnie was helping me dress today. She was ashamed of what she saw and said I had disgraced our family. We told Father after dinner tonight. Bellowing, Father asked who had done this to me. After I had told him, he began pacing the room. Mother sat with Bonnie, and both were crying silently.

    Poor Weston was in utter bewilderment that he had not realized my condition. Father brought Thomas into the house and demanded he leave the property by dawn. Thomas was concerned about Virginia, but Father said she would not be punished for her brother's sin and that she may stay. I protested and told Father that Thomas did not force himself on me. Thomas said he loved me and wanted to marry me. Father told us we do not know love—only sin and lust. When I disagreed with Fa-

145

ther, I thought he would strike me had Thomas not been standing between us.

Thomas agreed to leave immediately without pay for this week. As he left, he said Romeo and Juliet made the right decision by defying their families. Father ordered me to my room and told me to stay there until morning. He said he could not bear to look at me until then. I saw Thomas one last time only moments ago. I told him how much I love him. He said the same before we embraced and kissed for the last time before his departure. I gave him a letter detailing plans for our reunion. It is forever until then. I wish my love would wait until morning to leave, but I understand why he cannot stay here any longer.

30 August 1846

Upon waking this morning, I found that Thomas left his mother's jewelry case beside my bed sometime during the night. Inside it was the letter I gave to him last night. I fear he never read my words, but I pray he did, for if he did not I might never see him again. I took the case back to the lighthouse hoping last night had been a nightmare. I had hoped to find Thomas sleeping, but his bed was empty.

6 September 1846

Father has told everyone I have left Bettencourt to visit relatives in the north. Meanwhile, I am forbidden to leave the grounds until after my child is born. Weston will be my doctor. I will not be lonely, for Bonnie is no longer able to travel into town. She is experiencing more difficulty with her pregnancy than I am with my own.

Though Mother insists no one in town knows of my condition, I feel she is lying. There must be a few souls who find it peculiar that the firing of Thomas coincides with my disappearance. Perhaps some think Thomas and I have run away to be married because Father does not approve.

22 October 1846

I miss Thomas more than I thought possible. Yesterday, Father announced plans for the introduction of my child into the family. He has asked that Weston and Bonnie raise my child along with their own, letting everyone believe the children are twins. I shall marry Sebastian as planned, telling him nothing. Reluctantly, Bonnie and Weston agreed to spare the family of embarrassment.

I sobbed at the thought of giving up my child. As much as I fear her arrival, I cannot leave her and pretend that she is only a niece, or nephew if my instincts are wrong and the child I carry is male. Later, I spoke with Weston and Bonnie alone. I told them of my plans to leave with Thomas after my child is born. They understood my decision, for they know how one feels when in love. Both have agreed to keep my plan secret and pretended to accept Father's request. Should he learn of my plans, he will never know I have confided in Weston and Bonnie.

18 November 1846

Mother is kind to me now that I have agreed to let Bonnie raise my baby. Bonnie feels her child is a boy just as distinctly as I feel mine is a girl.

I collapsed in pain this morning. Weston tells me if I do not rest, my child will be born too early. My child might not live if she is born now. I am so frightened. I wish Thomas could be here with me. He would know how to ease my mind of such terrible fears. At least I will be able to knit baby clothes while I am confined to my bed for the next month. As I lie here, I feel her moving inside me. I love her even though I have never met her.

2 December 1846

Weston tells me my child will arrive soon. It does seem rather odd to have my sister's husband examine me. Every moment of thought I give to Father's decision leaves me in a moment of pain, for my child kicks me. I completed the baby's blanket and doll last week. I only lack completion of the dress.

Because I am confined to my bed, I have begun to consider names for my daughter. As of now, I feel a name from a Shakespeare play will be a name Thomas shall approve of. He had told me before he left that any name I chose for our child would please him. Perhaps our child will be named Ophelia, or Juliet. I have considered other names, those of my childhood friends Lucietta and Antoinette, or perhaps Elberta after my grandmother. No matter what I call her, she is loved.

12 December 1846

Just after dawn yesterday, I gave birth to my daughter. She is a perfect child, so angelic and beautiful. I thought I would die from the pain before she arrived. Her name shall be Antoinette Elberta, for Weston and Bonnie agreed to let me name her. Antoinette has dark hair, like that of my dear Thomas. Her eyes are blue now but might turn brown like mine.

I wish Thomas were here to see what our love has created. Our plans are only wrong because I shall never see my family again. How I wish Father would reconsider and allow me to marry Thomas with his blessing. I will send a letter to Sebastian soon to break our engagement.

When Thomas comes for me after Christmas, I will go with him and leave behind all I have known for seventeen years. No one will know I am gone until the next morning because we plan to leave during the late evening.

Chapter 20

I couldn't believe what I had just read. Bo and I skimmed through the entries again to try to get a better feel for Caroline's state of mind leading up to her death. Nothing in the diary led me to believe she had been suicidal. The most astonishing discovery was that Antoinette had belonged to Caroline, not Bonnie.

The diary confirmed what I already knew in my heart; it had been Caroline's portrait I'd found. I looked just like her.

"Wow," Bo said. "That was intense."

"My brothers and I are descendants of Caroline, not Bonnie. If she and Thomas hadn't gotten carried away, we wouldn't exist. And we're also the only surviving family members of Caroline."

"She didn't write like someone who would commit suicide, but we don't know what might have happened after her last entry," Bo said. "And what about Thomas? We don't know what he was thinking or why you saw his spirit in the boathouse."

"Well, there's no note, but she was desperate to be with Thomas," I said. "Everything was tearing them apart and with all her emotions from the pregnancy…"

"Do you still think it's her spirit you felt in this room?" Bo asked.

"Yes, without a doubt," I said. "I feel like she's been feeding me some of her memories. I can see Thomas' face in my mind as clearly as I see yours. It's how I knew just now about the trunk bottom. I think she led me to this. I have to see those newspapers and figure out what she wants. She's the only spirit I haven't actually seen."

"And the boathouse?" Bo asked.

"I don't know," I said as I got up. "Let's talk to Jon now."

We walked to my brothers' room, and I knocked on the door. Brad said we could come in. Jon was lying on his bed, looking out the window and Brad was sitting in a chair near the fireplace and looked like he had been deep in thought. Bo sat on the end of Brad's bed, and I went to sit by Jon. He looked angry and frightened.

"I'm fine," Jon said, not giving me time to ask.

"I need your help, Jon," I said. "You're the only one who can help Thomas move on. I can't go in the boathouse. From what I saw, he was in terrible shape."

"I just need a bit longer to deal with this," Jon said as he sat up. "I'm freaking out here."

"Okay," I said. "But there's more. Bo and I found Caroline's diary in my room. We read through most of it and learned a few things."

"What?" Brad asked.

I handed the diary to him. "It was at the bottom of the trunk," I said. "She and Thomas were truly in love. She wrote about how they sinned."

"Sinned?" Brad asked.

"Serena was right. Caroline got pregnant," I said. "The baby was Antoinette, who Bonnie raised as her own child."

"Antoinette," Jon said. He muttered something else I couldn't understand.

"One of the entries is about posing for the portrait," I said. "That painting upstairs proves that I look just like her. And Mom's bracelet—it's the same one Caroline is wearing in the portrait."

"Shit!" Brad said. "Did she leave a suicide note in here?"

"No," I said. "But we don't know what she was thinking in the end because the diary stops right after she gave birth. She probably had a pretty rough recovery. They didn't have the drugs we have now."

"She wrote a lot about how much she loved Thomas," Bo said. "They planned to run away together. As much as she loved him, I don't think she would have killed herself and left their baby behind."

"I have to see the newspapers at the library to see what is written about their deaths," I said. "I'm wondering if her death wasn't just a terrible accident. I think Bo's right; I don't see how she would decide to leave the baby behind."

"I know Justy will help us," Bo said.

"I'll go to the boathouse," Jon said. "But you have to stay away, Caroline. Let's go, Brad. Let's get this done. I can't handle much more of this."

"I'm game," Brad said. "Ready for ghostbusting."

I couldn't help but laugh, but I felt bad about it.

Bo and I watched my brothers from the window in their room. They walked down the hill toward the boathouse. When they arrived, Jon stood back and kicked the door a couple of times. I saw the ice break off and fall to the ground around it. Brad joined with the kicking, and the two of them were able to get the door open. They went inside while I stood in front of the window watching and waiting.

"I'm scared," I said. "Virginia's spirit wasn't harmful, but what if this one is?"

Bo stood behind me and wrapped his arms around me. "I think everything is going to be fine," he said. "Remember what Aunt Serena said. She didn't feel like the spirits here were harmful."

"But, what if she's wrong?" I asked as I turned around to face Bo.

"I've never known her to be wrong about stuff like that," he said.

"I can't just stand here," I said. "Let's go downstairs."

Margo and Marlene were in the kitchen heating up leftovers for dinner. They had pans on each of the burners on the cooktop and things in both wall ovens. They were talking about how much easier it would be with a microwave.

Marlene noticed the necklace around my neck as soon as she saw me. She came over and picked it up off my chest. "This looks like it was made for you, sweetheart," she said. "I knew it was too girly for Bo when I gave it to him. I'm so glad he chose to give it to you." She hugged me.

"I love it," I said. "It's beautiful."

Margo inspected the necklace. "That's very special," she said. She winked at me. "We've been gossiping all day, what have you two been up to?"

Bo and I looked at each other but didn't say anything as we sat down at the bar. Marlene and Margo looked back and forth at us.

"We were talking about your mother, Caroline, and I told Margo a little about a séance we had here a long time ago. Do you know about that?" Marlene asked.

"I know now, but I didn't before I came here," I said. "Serena told me about it, and I found a diary Mom kept with an entry about it."

"Bob and I never told Bo about that night either," Marlene said. "To be honest, it really scared me."

"Caroline," Margo said. "I'm sorry to have broken your trust, but after Marlene told me about the séance, I told her about what you saw in the stable."

"Oh," I said. "That's okay. It's all over now. I talked to Serena about it, and she told me what to do, so the ghost in the stable has moved on."

"Well, I'm glad that's all over," Margo said. "Has anything else happened? Supernatural, I mean?" She went back to the oven to check on the food.

I didn't want to tell them what else was going on with the spirits. I looked at Bo and could tell he understood not to say anything about what Brad and Jon were doing or what we had found in my room. Bo put his hand over mine under the counter and gave it a squeeze.

Bo leaned over and whispered in my ear while his mom and Margo had their backs turned. "Do you think your brothers are okay?"

By the time he had finished asking, both ladies had turned around and were looking at me. As sweet as our new romance was to me, I knew we couldn't keep it a secret forever. I pulled mine and Bo's hands out from under the counter and laid them on top, leaving our fingers intertwined. Bo didn't seem to mind because he kept holding my hand. Both ladies noticed immediately and reacted by squealing and jumping up and down.

"Oh, it's about time!" Marlene said. "All this boy has done is talk about you since Mark and Margo's wedding."

"Oh God," Bo said. "Mom, please stop."

"Don't be embarrassed," Marlene said. "We already know. We saw you two kissing by the lighthouse earlier."

"You what?" Bo asked. His face was as red as mine felt.

"Bob was showing the kids how the clouds move over the ocean. He called us over. We couldn't help but see," Marlene said. "Roberta and I used to say all the time when you two were little that we hoped you'd get together someday. You've always been so cute together—best friends."

"Okay, now I'm really embarrassed," Bo said.

So far, none of the kisses we had shared had been private, and our mothers had discussed us long ago.

"Please tell me Dad didn't see," I said.

Margo didn't answer. She just smiled, then turned away from me and began taking food out of the oven. I glanced back at Bo.

"There are the two lovebirds," Dad said from behind me. "Where are your brothers?"

I put my head down on the counter and wondered if it was possible to die from embarrassment. I wanted the floor to open up and swallow me. Bo released his grip on my hand. I didn't bother raising my head because Bo answered for me.

"They're fixing the boathouse door, Mr. Douglas," he said. "We'll go get them for dinner, sir."

Bo grabbed my hand again and dragged me out of the kitchen. I was worried that Jon and Brad were not back yet.

"I'm sorry," Bo said when we got to the entryway. "I can't believe they all just stood there at the window watching us."

"It's fine," I said. "We can't change it. And I don't think my dad's going to kill you or anything since you're all 'Mr. Douglas' and 'Sir' with him now."

"Well, I can't exactly call my girlfriend's dad Uncle Mark anymore. That's just too weird."

He had called me his girlfriend. It was starting to feel real to me.

"Come on," I said. "Let's go outside."

Bo looked around and then quickly kissed me. "There," he said. "Privacy." He took my hand and opened the door for me.

Jon and Brad were on the porch when we stepped outside. Brad was standing at the top of the steps, and Jon was sitting with his back against the house. Jon had his head between his knees and was taking deep breaths trying to calm down. I looked at Brad, who nodded at me. The sun was beginning to set; it would be dark soon.

I stood by Jon and touched his head. "Are you okay?" I asked.

He raised his head and wiped tears off his face with his forearm. I was shocked to see him crying. I dropped to my knees in front of him.

"Jon, what happened?" I asked. I looked up at Brad. "Brad?"

"He talked to the ghost, and it left," Brad said.

I stayed kneeling in front of Jon. The porch felt cold and hard on my knees, but I ignored it. I was extremely worried about my brother.

"I'll be fine," he said. "I just got hit with a lot of pain when he…"

"Pain?" I asked. "What kind of pain?"

"Does it matter?" Brad asked.

"Gut-wrenching physical pain," Jon said. "Like every bone in my body was broken."

"I'm so sorry," I said. "I shouldn't have asked you to go in there."

"As soon as I walked through the door, I heard gurgling and choking. He was choking on his own blood because the fall didn't kill him and somehow he managed to crawl to the boathouse. I'm glad I couldn't see him. He asked me if I knew the condition of Caroline. I told her she was dead and he was too and needed to move on.

"Then he asked about Virginia, so I told him what happened to her and said she was waiting for him on the other side. He told me he and Caroline planned to run away together with the baby and Virginia the day after Christmas. The snowstorm left Thomas stranded outside of town so he wasn't able to get to the estate until a few days later. After the

156

snow had stopped, he came for Caroline, but he was told Caroline and the baby had died."

"But that's not true," I said.

"We know it's not true, but that's what the Marshalls' servant told him," Jon continued. "After hearing the news, Thomas climbed to the top of the lighthouse and intended to jump. He said something startled him from behind and when he turned around he saw Caroline. She told him not to jump. Seeing her caused him to lose his footing and fall to the ground through a loose railing.

"He was still waiting for Caroline because he thought the servant had lied to him about her death. I told him his baby lived, had a family, and grew old before she died. I said she and Virginia would be waiting for him and Caroline would be there soon if he would just move on. I couldn't hear him anymore after that. Then all the pain hit me."

"I felt his spirit leave at that point," Brad said. "I didn't feel physical pain, but I felt a whole lot of sadness. Then I had to drag Jon out of there because he kind of fell apart."

"Jon, can you stand?" Bo asked. "We need to get you inside; the wind is picking up out here."

Bo was right; I was so engrossed in Jon's story I hadn't noticed it was dark outside and getting much colder.

We helped Jon to his feet and got him into the house. As soon as we got him under the light in the entryway, I realized how pale he was. Not wanting to freak out the adults, I made up a lie on the spot that Jon had slipped on some ice. It had to be serious enough to keep him off his feet for a little while, but not serious enough to cause a trip to the hospital.

No one questioned my story because everyone was too busy talking about how cute Bo and I had looked kissing by the lighthouse. We were a united front for the humiliation we endured during dinner but were not too embarrassed to be holding hands under the table. Hearing the words "boy-friend" and "girlfriend" used to describe us still seemed strange to me. I thought dinner would never end.

Trini came to my room later that evening. My door was open, so she stood in the hallway before I motioned for her to come in. She ran to the bed and jumped up on it to sit with me.

"What's up kid?" I asked. "Have you had a good Christmas?"

"Yes," she said as she grinned and bounced on the bed. "I am so glad Santa found us here."

"Of course," I said. "Santa always knows where you are." I couldn't remember when I had learned the truth about Santa. I might have been just a little older than her. I figured it was best to keep the magic alive for as long as possible.

"Did you wish for a kiss from Bo for Christmas?" she asked. "Do you love him? Are you going to marry him?"

I was glad Trini hadn't asked those questions during dinner when everyone else was asking us our intentions.

"Yes, I love him, and I don't know, Trini," I said. "Maybe I'll marry him someday. I'm too young to get married right now."

"How old do you have to be to get married? Older like Mom and Dad?"

"Eighteen, legally," I answered. "But that's still very young."

My answer seemed to satisfy her.

"If you marry Bo, will he be my brother?"

"Sure," I said.

"And if you have a baby what will it be to me?"

I laughed. "Your niece or nephew," I said. "But, there won't be any babies for a very long time. I'm too young for that."

"How long is a very long time?" she asked.

"I don't know," I said. "Ten years?"

"Okay," she said. She hopped off the bed and ran down the hallway to her room.

Sometimes I missed being as innocent as Trini. But growing up had its advantages too. I had a boyfriend. Bo was my boyfriend, which was wonderful.

I felt some relief from the feeling of doom I had sensed earlier in the week when I crawled into bed. I wore the necklace Bo had given me and once again prayed for a peaceful night. I promised Caroline I would try to help her reunite with Thomas and their daughter if she could just let me sleep.

Chapter 21

December 26, 1996

I woke up at dawn and felt like I had slept well. I looked out my window at the silhouette of the lighthouse against the sunrise. It amazed me how something of such great beauty might hold within its walls the answers to the biggest mystery I had ever encountered. I felt like I was running out of time to figure out how to help Caroline. I hoped Justice would be willing to let me see the newspaper articles at the library later in the day.

After breakfast, Jon and Brad led the kids on a treasure hunt through the house in search of the key to the lighthouse. They used the engineer's scheduled arrival on Monday as an excuse to find the key so the old lock might be spared. Jack and Trini were up to the challenge and looked in every possible hiding spot they could think of.

Bo called after breakfast to ask if I could go with him and Justice to the library. Dad agreed to let me go. They arrived in her car mid-morning to pick me up.

"So she's giving you some of her memories," Justice said after I had described some of my dreams to her. "It sounds like she's latching on to you—like how you almost introduced yourself as her when I first met you. She's trying to get in your head."

"I guess so," I said. "It's weird how all of a sudden, I just know things—like the bottom of the trunk being false. I remember a spiral staircase now, but I know it's not something I've seen before."

"That's how a lot of the things I know come to me," Justice said. "I can't explain it."

"Maybe the staircase you're remembering is inside the lighthouse," Bo said.

"I don't know," I said as we pulled up to the library. "It was too dark to tell. I can still see Thomas' face and feel the love she had for him. It hurts, but feels better the farther away I get from the estate."

The library was a two-story red brick building with five windows on the top floor. Four white columns embellished the front entrance below a dome-shaped center window. Justice drove to the back entrance and parked in the employee area, which was hidden from the street. We had to leave most of the lights off so no one would think the building was open for business. She locked the door behind us and led us to the room with the film readers. She left to retrieve the film.

Bo turned to me. "Caroline," he said. His voice was low, and he sounded unsure of himself. "You said you could feel the love the other Caroline felt for Thomas. You're not projecting her feelings onto me, right? I mean, do you still have feelings for me today now that you're away from the house?"

I walked over to him and wrapped my arms around his waist. "Bo, I'm not confusing my feelings with hers," I said. "I promise I still love you when I'm away from the house."

"I'm sorry," Bo said. "I guess I still can't believe it's true." He smiled, then kissed me.

Justice walked back into the room and cleared her throat to get our attention. "Guys," she said. "I found the film."

Bo let go of me, and we sat down at the film-reading computer. Justice had returned with a few boxes of film of the Bettencourt Ledger from 1847-48. She turned on the machine and loaded the film for me. The first paper from 1847 had a full-page article about the deaths of Caroline and Thomas and a birth announcement for Antoinette and Weston. A June paper covered the deaths of the Marshalls and Virginia. The January 1848 paper referenced the lights at the lighthouse.

January 6, 1847

Tragic Double Suicide at Bettencourt Estate

In the early morning hours of December 27, Miss Caroline Ellen Marshall, aged 17 years, committed suicide by jumping from the Bettencourt lighthouse. She died instantly from a broken neck. Miss Marshall was engaged to Mr. Sebastian Collierman, III. A letter from Miss Marshall to Mr. Collierman to break their engagement was discovered at the town post office after her death. The post was delayed by the recent blizzard. Miss Marshall was the daughter of Mr. and Mrs. Colin Marshall and the granddaughter of the late Mr. and Mrs. Campbell Bettencourt. Survivors include her parents, her sister, Mrs. Weston Brown, a nephew, Master Weston Brown, Jr. and a niece, Miss Antoinette Brown.
In a shocking turn of events, a second suicide occurred at the same location in the days after. Mr. Thomas W.

Cooper, aged 18 years, former lighthouse caretaker, jumped from the lighthouse on December 29. He died from his terrible injuries in the estate's boathouse the next day. Mr. Cooper left his post in August and was rumored to have been the lover of the late Miss Marshall. He is survived by his sister, Virginia Cooper, who is being cared for by the Marshall family.

Twins for Dr. Brown

Twins born to Dr. and Mrs. Weston Brown December 26. Son, Weston Brown, Jr., and Daughter, Antoinette Brown.

June 16, 1847

Tragedy continues at Bettencourt Estate

A stable fire claimed the lives of Mr. and Mrs. Colin Marshall and Miss Virginia Cooper late evening June 10. Their bodies were discovered with the livestock during the early morning hours of June 11. The estate was the location of a tragic double suicide of the Marshall's youngest daughter, Caroline, and her lover, Thomas, just six months ago.

January 5, 1848

Mysterious lights at Lighthouse

Rumors are circulating in town of the long-closed light-house operating again. Various residents saw a light from the lighthouse during the late evening hours of December 26 and the early morning hours of December 27. The lighthouse was closed after a tragic double suicide one year ago. A new lighthouse was constructed up the coast but is not responsible for the light seen in Bettencourt. The sheriff is investigating claims of witchcraft and trickery.

"There are a few more reports scattered in the next few years similar to the first one about the lights in the light-house," Justice said. "But you get the idea."

"This reads like a tabloid," I said. I was still reeling from the details.

"It's how things were done in newspapers back then," Justice said. "Scandals sold papers. This one still runs once a week, although it's not quite as sensational now. Bake sales and scout camping trips—your basic small town stuff. They don't even cover the lighthouse lights anymore, but they do still hold a 'man on the street' question about it every few years or so to keep the legend alive."

"Still running?" I asked. "Do you think they would print a retraction or a correction to the original article if I provided them with proof that Caroline didn't commit suicide?"

"Maybe," Justice said. "Mom's best friend is the publisher. She would probably want to run excerpts from the diary. Would you be willing to share it with her?"

"I'd be willing to share photocopies with her," I said. I pulled the diary out of my purse. I had carefully wrapped it in a towel to protect it. "Could we copy it here?"

Justice was amazed by its pristine condition. "May I hold it?" she asked.

I handed it to her.

Justice held it and closed her eyes for a moment. "There is so much pain in here," she said. "But I agree with you that what you told me so far does not indicate someone who was suicidal. You have to contact her spirit and find out what happened after the last entry. I think she'll move on if you clear her name."

"How do we help our Caroline do that?" Bo asked. He was printing copies of the newspaper articles for me to share with my brothers.

"We need to help her get inside the lighthouse. I think the answer is there," Justice said. "I'll come back with you to help if you want me to."

"Yes, please," I said. I definitely needed her help. I watched while Justice made copies of the diary.

Bo put his arm around me. "This is going to end tonight," he said.

"I have to run to my house first to pack an overnight bag," Justice said when she had finished making the copies.

"Do you really think it'll take all night?" I asked.

"No," she said. "But we're going to be snowed in until at least tomorrow afternoon until the snowplows can clear everything."

There had been no new snow during the last couple of days. The weather station had predicted only a twenty percent chance for the evening.

Bo noticed my confusion. "She's usually pretty accurate when she's dreamed about something," he said. "I've just gotten used to her weirdness."

Justice laughed. "I dreamt about it last night," she said. "It won't be too bad, but we'll be stranded for the evening. At least a foot of snow I think. I wish I could choose what I dream about, but random things usually just come to me. Sometimes they're important, and sometimes not."

After a quick trip to Justice's house, we stopped by the cemetery with a copy of the plot records. Justice pointed out the grave that belonged to Caroline Marshall. It was the same one I had felt so strongly about on Christmas Eve. Nearby were the graves of Thomas and Virginia. Their stones had also become smooth with age. Only a few letters and numbers could be read.

We went to the newer part of the cemetery to pay our respects to my great-grandparents. Their headstone was a flat joint one with a vase in the middle above the name "Levy." It contained new silk poinsettias.

"Who did this?" I asked.

"My mom," Bo said. "She keeps it decorated when she decorates our family's graves."

"That's so nice," I said. "And thoughtful."

"She liked them very much," Bo said. "She practically lived at their house during the summers when your mom was here."

"Maybe Caroline wants a better headstone," I said. "Like what your friend said at the beach."

"Her stone isn't like the others because her family was ashamed, thinking she had committed suicide," Justice said. "That's why she's buried outside of the family plot. I don't know how Thomas came to be buried right beside her, but I think Bonnie had Virginia buried next to them. I just love the history in cemeteries. They speak so much about the time periods with how the stones were carved and the graves laid out. It's fascinating."

"I've always loved history, too," I said. "I want to teach it someday."

Justice smiled. "I think I'll still do some research on the side even when I'm a nurse," she said. "I care a lot about this old town and all the legends."

It was sad to me that Caroline and Thomas couldn't be together in life, but at least their bodies were together in death.

Chapter 22

I was disappointed no one had found the key to the light-house while we were gone. My brothers were in the living room talking about it with Dad when Bo, Justice, and I got back.

"We've looked just about everywhere," Brad said. "I don't know where else to look."

"We'll just have to call a locksmith," Dad said. "They might be able open the lock without breaking it."

"Yeah," Jon said. "They'll pick it with a hairpin and charge you a lot of money. We could do that if we had a hair-pin."

"This house is almost two hundred years old," Justice said. "It's a safe bet there's a hairpin in here somewhere."

Bo and I laughed.

Jon laughed too. "I didn't think of that," he said.

Jack screamed from the entryway. "I found it!" he said. "I think I found the key!" He was holding a key that looked similar to the one I had found that opened the trunk.

"Where did you find it?" I asked. I noticed the top of the newel post was missing at the bottom of the stairs.

"Right here," he said. He showed us the empty cavity inside the banister. "I was coming downstairs, and I noticed it was loose. Then the whole top came off."

"Good job," Dad said. "I think you just saved us lock-smith money."

Jack beamed with pride. "Can we go see if it works?" he asked.

"Yes," Dad said. "But no one goes up the stairs until the engineer comes next week. I don't want any accidents."

Dad and Margo had planned to take the kids to see a movie that evening, but really only Trini wanted to go. We were fine with Jack staying behind with us because we knew he would be no trouble. I felt deceitful not telling them about the snow Justice predicted, but I knew we would have a better chance of accomplishing our mission without Dad and Margo around.

We grabbed our coats and headed for the lighthouse as they were leaving. The lighthouse was not that far away from the house, but it felt like an eternity passed before we got there. The cold air felt extremely heavy and wet as we made our way across the yard. I glanced up at the dark, cloudy sky and expected snow to fall at any moment. I was shivering before Bo put his arms around me and stood to block the wind.

Jon shined a flashlight on the lock. We let Jack try to open it since he had found the key. I held my breath as Jack tried to turn the key. The lock would not open even though the key seemed to be a perfect fit.

"Maybe it's not the right key," Brad said.

Jon examined the lock. "It is the right key," he said. "The lock is just stuck."

Jon took a can of lubricant out of his coat pocket and sprayed the lock using the little tube that was attached to the can. He removed a lot of gunk from the lock, but it still wouldn't budge.

Bo looked at the lock more carefully and confirmed it had rusted too badly to be opened with a key or anything else.

The door also opened outward, which I thought was odd. It couldn't be kicked in like the boathouse door.

"You'll have to drill this out," Bo said. "It's damaged too badly. I've seen this at other places. I don't have any of my dad's tools with me."

"Our drill isn't powerful enough," Jon said.

"What about the window?" Justice asked.

We looked up at a window above the door. It was at least ten feet off the ground.

"It doesn't open," Bo said. "Dad had me climb a ladder and check it last week. We could break the glass, but it's still quite a drop on the inside, and we'd need a rope ladder so we could get in and back out."

"No, we can't do that," I said. "There has to be a better way."

I felt discouraged. Nagging thoughts told me I had to get into the lighthouse sometime before the next morning, but I didn't want to destroy the lock or break the window.

"I'll spray the lock again and let it sit there," Jon said. "Maybe it'll loosen up."

Defeated, we went back to the house.

We gathered in the living room and snacked while we looked over the articles from the old newspapers. We revealed to Jack what had been happening. He seemed a little freaked out at first but handled the information fairly well.

"What are we going to do if you can't get into the lighthouse?" Jack asked.

"We might be able to try a repeat séance up in your room, Caroline, since there are six of us here," Justice said. "That's the only thing I can think of."

"I don't know," I said. I remembered something in the diary about a passage. "I think there's another way in…"

"What?" Jon and Brad asked at the same time.

"Something in the diary," I said as I looked at Bo. "Do you remember reading about a passage?"

"Maybe," Bo said. "I can't read as fast as you, so I just skimmed it."

"A passage?" Justice asked. "I can go out to the car and get the copy of the diary."

"No, I'll go upstairs to get it," I said. "Will someone please go check the lock again?"

My brothers went outside as I ran upstairs to get the diary. I sat on my bed and used a flashlight to carefully look through the entries until I came across the one that mentioned the passage. Bo had followed me to my room.

"Here it is," I said. "It's the entry from May 30, the same one where she suspects she's pregnant."

Bo read over my shoulder. "Yeah, I remember that, now," he said. "It took me a minute when I first read it to figure out what a monthly was. I felt really stupid when I realized what she meant."

I laughed then gave him a quick kiss. "Bo, that's so funny," I said.

He shrugged his shoulders.

I read the section of the diary to him. "Grandmother Elberta told me secrets about this house that even Mother does not know. I miss her so. Thomas is the only person who knows what she told me about the passage."

"So you think it's a passage to the lighthouse?" he asked.

"Where were the secret passages located in the other houses you've worked on?" I asked.

"A lot of them were underground tunnels from the basement to other buildings," he said. "But I don't remember seeing anything in this basement. Some were passages between interior rooms."

I looked out the window at the darkness and saw snowflakes accumulating on the window panes. "Hey, look," I said as I pointed at the window. "Just like Justice said."

The front door slammed as Bo and I went back downstairs. My brothers were in the entryway, covered in snow.

"It's really coming down out there," Jon said. "There's no sign of it stopping. There's at least four inches on the ground already."

"It's no use on the lock," Brad said. "We can't get it open."

I saw a flash of color and my eyes started hurting, but I tried to ignore it. "We have to go to the basement," I said. "Caroline mentions in her diary a passage and secrets about the house that her grandmother told her. I think there's another way to get into the lighthouse."

Everyone followed me through the kitchen to the basement stairs. We grabbed extra flashlights along the way because we knew the basement was sparsely lit. As soon as we reached the bottom of the stairs, we split up and began searching for any signs of a passage. It was the first time I had been to the basement. I hadn't realized the foundation had been rebuilt from its original state. Newer brickwork now supported the house. If there ever was a passage from the basement to the lighthouse, it was long since covered.

The phone rang upstairs. Jack ran to answer it while we looked around one more time in vain. My head was throbbing, and I was having trouble focusing my eyes. The last thing I had time for was a migraine. I needed my medicine.

"I don't think there's a passage from here," Justice said. "But something's not quite right. This basement isn't as large as the house. That wall right there seems too close. I think there might be something behind it."

She was pointing to a wall that seemed like it would be right under the living room instead of under the back part of the house. The basement was oddly shaped.

"It could be nothing more than extra support for that part of the house and the chimneys," Jon said. "Look over there. It's similar where the chimneys are for the other bedrooms and the dining room. All of this has been rebuilt anyway. Look at the cinder block."

Jon was right that the other wall was similar in look and feel.

"I guess you're right," Justice said. "Let's go upstairs and figure this out."

Jack met us at the top of the stairs. "Mom called," he said. "They're staying at Bob's house. The snow is almost a foot already, and the plows won't run until morning. Bo, your dad wants you and Justice to stay here and not try to come home."

"As I predicted," Justice said.

As she finished speaking, the electricity went out. The darkness was comforting to me.

"But you didn't predict that," Jon said.

"It's not like I can turn it on and off like a television," she said. "You've come around to believing in the spirit world, pretty boy. Why can't you wrap your head around someone having random premonitions?"

Jon sighed. "I give up," he said.

Brad tried to stifle his laughter, but couldn't. "Can't you just feel the tension between them?" he whispered to me.

We used our flashlights to light the way up the stairs and gathered in the dining room.

"We need to get all the firewood and put it in the living room," Jon said. "If we all sleep in there, we can stay warm, and we'll only need one fire. I don't want to go outside again for more wood with that much snow unless we have to."

"What about the heater?" Jack asked.

"The blower won't work without electricity," Bo said. "The fireplace should keep us warm enough."

Jon put out his hand for Justice to take. "Miss, will you please help me with the firewood?"

She shook her head, but then placed her hand in Jon's and went upstairs with him. Jack and Brad grabbed the wood from the dining room. The light from the flashlight on the table was too bright. My head was throbbing with more intensity, and my eyes began to water. I felt more and more unsteady on my feet and stumbled into one of the dining room chairs.

"Hey," Bo said as he brushed my cheek with his fingers. "What's wrong?"

"I need to lie down," I said. "It's my head. I have medi-cine in my purse upstairs. I need some water. Help me, please."

Bo knew about my migraines and immediately helped me sit down in the dining room. I laid my head on the table while he went to the kitchen to get me a glass of water. When he came back, he helped me up the stairs and into my bed. He dumped the contents of my purse on the floor and sifted through everything until he found my medicine. After I had swallowed the pill, I curled up on the bed and tried to wait out the pain while Bo built a fire. Sometimes the medicine could take up to an hour to work, and even then, it often left me feeling exhausted.

I heard Bo talking to my brothers in the hallway while I had a pillow pulled over my head to block out the light from the fire.

"I don't care what your dad will think; I'm not leaving her in there alone," he said. "One of you can stay if you don't trust me."

"It's fine," Jon said. "We'll be downstairs. There's enough wood for both fires."

"Just let us know if she gets worse," Brad said.

Bo came back into the room and closed the door quietly. He sat in the desk chair beside the bed. I opened my eyes, but they were so watery I had trouble seeing.

"What can I do?" he whispered.

"I'm so cold," I said. Even with the fire and two blankets I still felt chilled to the bone and couldn't stop shivering.

"I'll get you another blanket," he said as he stood up.

"No, don't leave," I said as I reached for him. "Just hold me, please. I'll be okay soon."

Bo took off his boots and crawled into bed with me. He was careful not to jostle me too much. He stayed on top of the blankets and laid his head on the pillow that was propped against the headboard. He gently pulled me into his arms.

My tears dropped onto his shirt, leaving it damp beneath my face. Usually, I wanted to be left alone during a migraine, but listening to Bo's breathing and heartbeat helped take my mind off the pain because both had different rhythms than the throbbing in my head. I concentrated on his heart, counting the beats to stay distracted.

Jon came in later to check on me. "How's she doing?" he asked quietly.

"She's finally asleep," Bo whispered. "She stopped crying a little bit ago."

I wasn't asleep. The pain was better, but I didn't feel like getting up or admitting to them I was awake. I could have stayed there with Bo forever.

"Good," Jon whispered. "I'll come back in a couple of hours to check on the fire so you won't have to wake her."

"Thanks," Bo said.

"Do you need a blanket?"

"No, man, I'm good."

I heard Jon walk out and close the door behind him. Before long, the pain was completely gone.

Chapter 23

When I woke up, I felt better but didn't know where I was for a moment. The room was dark except for a few glowing embers from the fire. I was warm, and my head was still resting on Bo's chest. I reached up and touched his face.

Bo was asleep, but quickly stirred when I tried to sit up. He sat up and grabbed the flashlight and his glasses off the nightstand.

"Are you okay?" he asked. He shined the flashlight on the floor to keep it out of my eyes.

"I feel better," I said. "How long did we sleep?"

Bo shined the flashlight on his watch. "It's barely 11:00," he said. "So just a couple of hours."

He got up and put more wood on the fire. After he had stoked it, the fire brightened the room again. As I watched Bo, my eyes drifted to the bookcase. I was able to focus again. I had dreamlike memories of opening the bookcase like a door. Behind it was the spiral staircase I had dreamed about; I was sure of it. I glanced out the window and saw a faint light coming from the lighthouse. It wasn't much brighter than a candle, but it was definitely coming from the inside. I saw the snow falling heavily in front of it.

"Bo, look at the lighthouse."

"Yeah," he said as he sat down to put on his boots. "It starts low and gets a bit brighter and then goes out in the morning."

"She's out there," I said. I got up and put on my boots. I was relieved my head no longer hurt, and I could stand without feeling dizzy. "You have to help me with the bookcase. I dreamed it opens."

We pulled on the bookcase with no luck and then removed everything from the middle shelves. At the back of the shelf, a piece of trim looked slightly out of alignment with the other pieces. I removed it and found a latch behind it. After I had pressed the latch, we managed to pull the bookcase open.

Cold air stung my face as I peered into the narrow void behind the bookcase. A spiral staircase like the one I had seen in my dreams led to holes in the ceiling and the floor. Dust and cobwebs covered the stairs, the particles visible in my flashlight's beam. I knew the staircases led to the other bookcases in the upstairs bedroom and the living room. I had Caroline's memories of climbing through the passage.

Bo and I carefully descended the stairs. As we reached the first floor, I heard my brothers and Justice talking in the living room. Justice was telling them that she felt like there was a void behind the bookcase.

We released the latch and used all of our weight to press against our side of the bookcase. It opened with a loud creak, which silenced their voices. As we entered the living room, Jack screamed and jumped over the back of the sofa. Jon and Brad were stunned and stood there with their mouths gaped open.

Justice was only mildly startled. "Maybe you should listen to me more often," she said. She crossed her arms and looked at Jon.

"You might be wrong someday!" Jon said.

"Not today!" Justice said. "I told you!"

"Maybe you can use your psychic powers to sense when to shut up!" Jon said.

Brad had been right earlier; I could almost see the tension between them.

"Enough!" I said. "We have to get to the lighthouse. It's glowing."

Jack came out from behind the sofa and looked out the window. "It is!" he said.

Bo called me back into the passage to show me a narrow door on the floor. It was all so familiar to me. I knew it led to an underground tunnel that would lead us to the lighthouse. I felt like I had already passed through the tunnel many times.

Bo pulled the door open and looked inside. "It's a brick tunnel," he said. "I think you're right. I think it leads to the lighthouse."

"We have to go inside," I said. I ran to get my coat and gloves.

"But, Caroline, your head," Jon said. "Shouldn't you rest longer?"

"I'm fine now," I said. "I'm going, who's going with me?"

Brad and Jon crawled into the tunnel to check it out. They returned a few minutes later after they had determined it was safe. Justice and Jack agreed to stay in the house. Bo followed me as I crawled down the wooden ladder to join my brothers. They all carried flashlights to light our way. The air inside the tunnel smelled old and stale. The walls and ceiling were constructed in an arch of red bricks, reinforced by thick wooden beams every few feet. The ceiling was barely tall enough for Jon and Bo to walk upright and they still had to duck to go under the beams. The bricks that lined the floor followed the slope of the land toward the lighthouse.

When we reached the end of the tunnel, another wooden ladder led up to a door in the ceiling. After checking the ladder's safety, they let me climb up first and push open the door. As I pushed it, the sides of a heavy grey rug draped over both sides of the trap door. I had to use all of my strength to open the door all the way and then I climbed into the lighthouse.

I shined my flashlight on the cylindered walls and the wooden staircase that went up farther than my light could reach. Empty oil lanterns lined the staircase walls. The whole place was dark and creepy. Across from the main door was a small cast-iron cook stove. Beside it was a simple wooden table with two plain chairs. Tucked underneath the bottom of the staircase was a small room. Inside the room was a single metal frame bed and wooden night table. On the table was a tiny white porcelain jewelry box with golden hinges and pink roses painted on it.

"Caroline!" Jon called from the tunnel.

I went back to the trap door. "I'm fine," I said. "But I'm going to need more light and oil for the lanterns."

My brothers went back to the house to get the supplies while Bo climbed into the lighthouse with me. I went to the bedroom and picked up the jewelry box. I opened it carefully and worried the hinges might snap. Inside was a folded letter, which I opened so we could read it.

29 August 1846

My dearest Thomas,

The events of the day have deeply disturbed me. What you said about Romeo and Juliet as you left has made me fearful. You must not have been suggesting that we take our lives for love. My dear, we have created the life that now grows strong inside me. To carry out such a drastic measure would be defying God. We have created life; therefore, we must live.

I know how we can be together, but it will mean leaving Bettencourt forever. I am willing to make that sacrifice for you, my love. Come for me the night after Christmas. I will wait for you with our child in the boat-house. We will then leave here never to return.

Should you not come for me that night, I will understand you have refused my intentions. I know it will be difficult to live without you. If we do not see each other again, please know Virginia will be looked after. Farewell to you my dear Thomas. I will love you as long as I live and perhaps beyond. Though we may not meet again, I know we shall walk together in heaven someday.

Your loving Caroline

"Caroline brought this back in here with her," I said. "Remember, she wrote about finding this box with her letter inside? She was worried that Thomas didn't read it."

"What do we do now?" Bo asked. "She wrote she was against suicide, but that doesn't mean she didn't change her mind under the circumstances."

Jon and Brad came up through the door carrying the lamp oil and more flashlights. We showed them the letter.

"I know what we have to do," I said. I placed the letter back in the box. "We have to light the lighthouse like Caroline tried to so many years ago. Maybe that's what she's still trying to do."

"I can't climb those stairs," Brad said. "It was hard enough climbing in here."

"I will," Jon said. "But just Caroline and me for now. We don't know how sturdy the floor is up there. Let's go."

Bo was reluctant to stay behind but understood it was something I had to do without him. "Be careful," he said. He gave me a quick kiss on the lips and didn't seem to care that we were standing in front of my brothers. "Promise me."

"I promise," I said.

I hugged Bo, then started up the stairs with Jon. We took each step with care. I began to think the stairs would go on forever. My legs ached by the time we reached the top.

The many lanterns, mirrors, and prisms at the top of the lighthouse took my breath away. I had never seen anything so magnificent. A glass lantern in the center of the room seemed to be projecting a low light from within. The nine lanterns along the walls all had wicks and low levels of oil. Our flashlight beams reflected off the mirrors behind the lanterns and revealed that the glass surrounding us was caked with snow.

"We have to light them," I said.

Jon handed me one of the two lighters he had brought with him. We each tried several times to get the lanterns going, but the lighters would not stay lit long enough to light the wicks.

"We might have better luck with the long fireplace matches," Jon said. "They're still inside the house."

"I'll be fine here if you want to go get them," I said. "Maybe she'll talk to me if I'm alone."

"I'll be right back," he said. "Just stay here and don't do anything."

As soon as Jon was gone, the lanterns in the lighthouse lit up all at once. I turned in a complete circle to look at everything and had the distinct feeling I was not alone. When I turned around again, my ancestor—and mirror image—was standing in front of me.

Chapter 24

December 27, 1996

Caroline Marshall stood in front of me with a somber expression on her face. She wore a charcoal-colored overcoat and black leather gloves. I could see her cornflower blue dress poking out from the bottom of her coat. Her long blond hair was in a single braid hanging from within her sleeping cap. She didn't appear transparent like Virginia had, but looked like another person standing there with me. I stared at her, wondering if I should be afraid, but I wasn't.

"Thank you," she said. "I have waited here for you. You must help me remove the ice for the light to be seen."

As she pleaded with me, I could feel her desperation and hear the sadness in her voice. Her brown eyes conveyed more sorrow than I had ever seen. She felt like a friend I had known my whole life—a kindred spirit. I wanted to hug her, but I kept my distance.

"I'll do anything I can to help you, Caroline, but you have to tell me what happened. Do you realize that you died a long time ago?" I asked.

"Mother and Father were late because of the heavy snow," she said. "I tried to keep the lighthouse lit for them to know that we were safe, and to allow my dear Thomas to find his way to me. I wanted him to see the light and know I was waiting for him.

"The light was not bright enough because the windows were covered in ice, as they are now. I tried to scrape the windows, but I slipped on the ice and fell over the side. I tried to pull myself back to safety but did not have the strength. I fell. I felt intense pain for just a moment, and then it was gone. And I was back here, waiting, and I knew I was dead."

"Why didn't you move on?" I asked. I could feel pain radiating from her.

"I had to stay to tell Thomas about our daughter," she said. "When he came here, he was crying and about to jump. I called out to him. He turned and looked at me, then began to back away. I told him to stop, but he fell through the broken railing."

"Why are you still here?" I asked. I was saddened by her story.

"Thomas was still here, nearby but not reachable," she said. "Virginia too, but I cannot feel them now. I tried to communicate with others before you, but I could not reach them. I had to wait for you."

"Thomas and Virginia moved on," I said. "If you go too, you can be with them and Antoinette and the rest of your family."

"The light is not bright enough," she said. "Please help me remove the ice from the outside."

I thought about my brothers' dreams and my own dreams about falling. Against my better judgment, I followed her through a door that led to the outside ledge of the lighthouse. I used a blade I found inside and quickly scraped the layer of ice off the windows as snow fell heavily around me, which made it difficult to walk. When I had finished, the light shined brightly all around me. I was safe and ready to go back inside.

She took one last look at me and then vanished. As I felt her leave, more of her memories flooded my mind. I saw scenes of dancing with a tall man—the same man I had seen when I fainted in the stable. I recalled conversations with Bonnie and her parents, kissing Thomas, and holding a new-born baby.

When the memory of falling passed through me, I was overwhelmed and unintentionally took a step back. I felt my-self slipping on the ice. I screamed as I fell over the side and caught myself on the spindles below the broken railing. It was physically impossible to pull myself back to safety.

My mind was racing. I remembered a conversation be-tween my mother and grandmother when Granny Mavis had been in the hospital. They hadn't known I was in the hallway.

"Mom, you have so much to live for. Just keep fighting," my mother had said while standing at her mother's bedside.

"Dying is the easy part, all I have to do is let go," Mavis had said. "It's only hard for the people you leave behind."

Granny had died the next day.

I wasn't ready to die. I had so many people in my life to live for: Dad, my brothers and sister, Margo, Meema Douglas, Becca, and Bo. I loved them all so much; I couldn't leave them all behind.

"Don't let go," a sweet voice whispered inside my head. It was Mom's voice.

I tightened my grip and prayed for my safety. I screamed again for help.

"Caroline!" Brad and Bo screamed from inside the light-house.

Almost instantly, they were lying on the ledge with their legs still inside the lighthouse door. Brad seemed to have forgotten his fear of heights.

"Give me your hand," Brad said.

Bo had already grabbed my other wrist.

"I can't, or I'll fall," I said. "I can barely hang on. I'm slipping."

"Look at me!" Brad yelled. "I won't let you fall. Bo has your other hand. He won't let you fall."

"Never," Bo said. "I promise."

I listened to Brad, and within seconds he and Bo had pulled me to safety. My hands and arms were scraped and bleeding through my torn gloves and coat, but I was grateful to be alive. As I realized the seriousness of what had just happened, I started crying hysterically.

"You're okay," Bo said. He started crying, too, as he kissed me. He held me tightly as we sat on the lighthouse floor. His hands and arms were scraped and bleeding like mine.

"She was so scared," I said. "I felt her memories and everything she felt as she was falling. I think she's gone now."

Brad was crying too. "What the hell were you thinking?" he asked. "What were you doing out there? You could have died!" He was sitting up, holding his left shoulder. His hands were bloody.

"I'm sorry," I said. "It was an accident. The rail is broken."

Jon came running up the stairs. He dropped the matches and demanded to know what had happened. I told them about Caroline and how ultimately neither she nor Thomas had committed suicide.

After I had calmed down, we went back to the house. We carefully began our descent with Bo helping me, and Jon helping Brad. Justice and Jack were at the entrance to the tunnel when we got back. They had seen the whole thing through the living room window.

Justice was our nurse as she practiced her planned future career, cleaning and bandaging our cuts. She couldn't make the deepest cut on my forearm stop bleeding after applying pressure to it for more than twenty minutes. Jack was so helpful running back and forth to the kitchen to bring more clean rags.

"If it weren't for the snow, we would need to go to the hospital," she said. "Is your tetanus shot up to date?"

"I think so," I said.

"I can't get the bleeding to stop," she said. "You're losing a lot of blood."

"It's the migraine medicine," I said. "It thins my blood."

"We can try gluing it closed with superglue," she said. "But if that doesn't work, we'll have to call for help and maybe the hospital can send a helicopter."

Justice used almost a whole tube of superglue. Once it started to dry a bit, she and Jon each pressed on one side of my cut to hold it closed. That was more painful than when I had gotten the cut in the first place. I clenched my teeth and waited to see if it would help. It worked. Once the glue had dried, my bleeding stopped. Justice put a tight bandage around my arm just to be sure.

"Brad, is your shoulder okay? Will it keep you from playing baseball?" I asked. I felt terrible.

He was sitting on the sofa near the fire with an ice pack laying on his shoulder. "I'll be fine," he said. "I pulled a muscle I think. Nothing's broken. Baseball doesn't matter. I'm just glad you're okay."

Bo had not left my side. He wouldn't let Justice touch his cuts until my mine were okay. His cuts were not as severe as mine or Brad's because his coat was leather and much tougher than the wool ones my brother and I were wearing.

"Do we need to get our stories straight for when Dad gets home?" Jon asked.

"No," I said. "I can't lie to him anymore. I have to tell him the truth about everything even if he doesn't believe me. It's all over now I hope."

"It is," Justice said. "There are no more spirits here. I felt her leave right before I saw you fall."

Jack came over and hugged me. "Please don't ever go to the top of the lighthouse again," he said.

"I won't," I said. "I promise."

We all stayed in the living room by the fire. Jack and Brad fell asleep sprawled out on the floor. Jon and Justice sat at the end of one sofa and quietly talked. The light in the lighthouse stayed bright for a few more hours until it became dimmer and dimmer and faded away.

Bo and I curled up in the oversized armchair and watched out the window until the sun began to rise. By that time, Justice had moved to the other sofa and she and Jon were both asleep. Bo and I were the only ones still awake. I had so much on my mind; I was afraid to go to sleep.

"Aren't you tired?" Bo whispered.

"I'm not sure what I am," I said. "Aren't you?"

"I was worried your arm might start bleeding again, so I made sure I stayed awake."

"Bo, the lighthouse…"

"What about it? Is it glowing again?"

"No," I said. "When I fell…the way I fell…I don't see how I grabbed that railing."

Bo pulled me closer and held my hand. "You can't keep thinking about it, or you'll never sleep again," he said. "Sometimes impossible things just happen."

"I heard Mom's voice. She told me not to let go."

"She must have known Brad and I were running up the stairs."

"Brad's afraid of heights, but you both saved me."

"He ran without stopping from the moment we heard you scream. I've never been so scared in my whole life."

"I'm sorry I put you and Brad in danger," I said. I figured I was completely out of tears at that point, but I wasn't.

"Don't cry, we're all okay," Bo said. He wiped the tears from my cheeks and kissed me softly. "Now try to get some sleep. I'll stay right here with you."

When Dad woke us later, it was late afternoon. The sun was shining brightly through the windows and was reflecting off the snow outside. I was still wrapped up in Bo's arms, and we had been asleep for hours. The view was spectacular. Everything looked pure and white, and the whole place felt peaceful.

Everyone else had gone into the kitchen to eat and left Bo and me sleeping. We hadn't noticed when the fire went out because sometime during the morning, the electricity had been restored and the heater began working again. None of us had heard the small snowplow Dad had followed down the driveway. It helped that Bob had a lot of friends with snowplows. According to Dad, the snow accumulation was around fifteen inches. Justice's dream had been fairly accurate.

Jack took Trini upstairs so we could tell Dad and Margo what had happened in the lighthouse. I couldn't tell if Dad believed us or if he thought we were all crazy as we recounted the ghost encounters and us helping them move on. He and Margo were horrified by what had happened at the top of the lighthouse but relieved I had not fallen. Dad praised Justice's efforts to patch our cuts, and then took us to the hospital to be checked out just to be safe.

The doctors at the small hospital clinic in town determined Justice had done a fine job with sealing and cleaning my largest cut and that it would cause more harm than good to bother it. Brad's shoulder injury was just a pulled muscle with no evidence of tearing. We each got new tetanus shots as a precaution. Bo's parents met us at the hospital to take him home. They were relieved that his injuries were superficial and that Brad and I would be fine.

By the time we got back to the house, I was exhausted. Dad followed me to my room to talk to me alone. He sat on the bed with me and looked at the bandages on my arms. The room was cold, so he built a fire. He stood staring at the fire with his back to me for a while, then covered his eyes with his hand and cried so hard his shoulders shook. I had not seen him cry like that since Mom's death.

"Daddy…" I said.

"Caroline," he said as he turned around to look at me. "Promise me you'll never do anything that stupid again. Don't keep things like that from me. Don't ever put yourself in danger. Climbing outside the lighthouse was extremely dangerous and stupid. I don't care how many ghosts told you to. She lost her life because of an accident. A stupid accident! Have you learned nothing in the last few years? Do you not realize how fragile your life is or what it would do to me or all of us if we lost you?"

He was right; I had never considered any of that. I had been incredibly selfish.

"I'm so sorry," I said. "I promise I'll be careful from now on." I got up to hug him and cried again.

Dad sat with me on the bed for a few minutes, then left me alone after that. It was the first time since we had arrived at the estate that I actually felt alone in the room. It was empty and cold, but calm, as it should be. I lay on the bed and thought about everything that had happened during the week. I knew my life would never be the same.

Epilogue

December 2016

The Bettencourt Estate B&B is a great success for my family. It is exactly what Dad had envisioned. We had the lighthouse restored and added an automated electric lens thanks to financial help from the town. We fixed the broken railing and permanently sealed the top door. The lighthouse has become a new beacon of hope for the community and has sparked more tourism to the area during the last twenty years. After the first two years, the whole place was so successful that we had the third floor renovated and plumbed to serve as more guest rooms.

After our first Christmas together, Bo spent his next two spring breaks with me, and I worked at the Bettencourt B&B so I could spend my next two summers with him. I loved Bo Russell with all of my heart. We shared so many firsts, and I regret nothing about our time together. The hardest first we shared was the true heartache we felt when we mutually agreed to break up at the end of the summer before my senior year in high school. Everything had grown much more intense between us that summer. The distance and traveling back and forth had gotten to be too much for us.

We both cried when he dropped me off at the airport before I left for home. It was only the second time I had seen Bo cry. We were still very much in love, but breaking up had been the right thing to do at the time. Bo had a full scholarship for a college near Bettencourt and a great job with his dad but would have given up both to move to be with me. I wanted to let him but thought he would regret it later if he left his home and threw away that part of his future. I wanted to experience my last year of high school without feeling like a piece of my heart was always somewhere else. I wasn't sure if our relationship could stand the test of time if we resented each other later for altering such major life decisions. We left with an understanding that it wasn't goodbye forever because we would always be friends even if we didn't get back together in the future.

I tried my best to be independent and even cut off my long hair to my chin, which made me barely recognize myself. I dedicated myself to school and did everything I could to stay busy, but there wasn't a single day that I didn't miss Bo. I worried that someday I would look back on our break-up as the worst mistake of my life and wondered if he felt the same way, but I never asked. In the back of my mind, I always hoped we would get back together someday when we were older.

We remained friends and spoke on the phone often. Neither of us dated anyone else seriously during that year. I couldn't because the thought had been too painful. My senior prom was especially bittersweet because the year before I had flown to Virginia for the weekend to go to Bo's prom with him. He offered to take me to mine and was upset when I declined since I had already agreed to go with a friend. We didn't speak again for a few weeks.

Bo rode with his parents to attend my high school graduation. I didn't know he was coming because I thought he was still mad at me about my prom. I had no idea how much seeing him would affect me. I had to give a speech in front of everyone because of my ranking in the class but felt like I was speaking only to Bo. Right before I walked on stage, I threw out the generic speech I had practiced countless times for my family. I looked down at the cross necklace Bo had given me, kissed it for luck, and then spoke from my heart.

"A word that comes to mind about preparing for life after high school is regret—avoiding it if we can. We all want to avoid regretting our major life decisions for careers, college, or love. We hope that everything we've learned up until now has prepared us for living our lives. We'll all take different paths, and some of us may never cross paths again, but if we all make a vow together right now to live without regret then we will always be united...as the class of 1999."

The tears I shed after my speech had nothing to do with feeling sentimental about graduating. I had a huge decision to make that I knew could affect the entire course of my life. I had been accepted to two universities. I had only a few weeks left to pick one and register for classes. One was mere minutes from my home, and the other was close to Bettencourt, twelve hundred miles away.

After the graduation ceremony, my family had planned a small party for me. Bo rode home with me because he said he wanted to talk. I wanted to talk to him too, but made only nervous small talk until I could make a quick stop at the cemetery where my mother was buried. I asked Bo to wait in the car. As I placed my graduation flowers on Mom's grave, I thought about how different my life might have been had she not died in the accident. I told her goodbye again that evening because I knew if there was any hope left in the world, my decision about college was already made.

When I turned around, Bo was walking toward me. I walked to him slowly, silently praying with each step that he still loved me as much as I loved him. Our eyes met, and I just knew he did.

We didn't say anything at first; we just embraced and shared the most passionate kiss we'd ever had. Tears followed, then we promised each other that being together was our only option from then on. I arrived at my own graduation party late because Bo and I sat at the cemetery and worked out our plans for who would be moving.

Bo didn't return to Bettencourt with his parents. He stayed with my family for the next week and helped me pack my things while I worked out some details. It made the most sense for me to move because I missed Bettencourt almost as much as I had missed Bo. The next weekend, Bo and I began our long drive to Bettencourt. Dad and Margo understood I wasn't just running away to be with Bo. I had a college scholarship, a job, and a place to live. I had a plan, despite how rebellious I felt. I had just turned eighteen, and I think they knew I would have gone with or without their approval. I thought about how different our situation was from that of Caroline and Thomas so many years ago. Having the support of our families was nice.

I lived and worked at the B&B that summer like I had for the previous two and attended college with Bo in the fall. I only traveled back home for holiday visits and the extremely difficult visit for Meema's funeral during my second semester. After that, I took summer classes with a plan to graduate with Bo in only three years.

During the summer before our last year at the university, Bo took me back to the same pavilion where we had shared our first kiss. We sat for hours talking about our plans for the upcoming year and what to do after graduation. Just as the sun began to set, Bo kneeled in front of me and proposed. A crowd had gathered on the beach nearby when they realized what was happening and everyone cheered for us when I accepted. There happened to be a photographer among the crowd that evening who captured the proposal for us. I treasure the photos from that day.

Bo and I were married in the church with the bell tower and had a reception at the Bettencourt Estate B&B the week after our college graduation right after my twenty-first birthday. Becca was my maid of honor. She told me she had known all along Bo and I would end up getting married someday. We hired the same photographer from the beach to capture our wedding memories. Although we were still very young, I felt like we had waited a lifetime by then.

Bettencourt became my home. I love living in a place with so much history for us. Like any couple, we've had our ups and downs throughout the years. It is nice to be able to go to the base of the lighthouse to talk whenever we have a disagreement and be standing at the place where we first declared our love for each other.

Five years into our marriage, I took Bo to the church bell tower to tell him I was pregnant. Later that year, I looked into the sweet face of our baby girl right after she was born and thought my heart might burst with all the love I felt for her and Bo. Annie looks like her grandmother Marlene with her dark hair, but she has blue eyes like Bo. Whenever Annie smiles or laughs, she reminds me of my mother. She is incredibly bright and shares my father's love for science. Her mind is always working. Annie amazes us every day. Justice says Annie has an old soul.

When our second daughter was born four years later, Bo said she looked exactly like me. When I compare Greta's baby pictures to mine, I see the similarities, and even though I never thought of myself as beautiful, I do see the beauty in her. Her mannerisms have become more and more like Bo's each day as she has grown. Greta is quiet and thoughtful like her father and is completely enamored with her big sister.

Jon's career turned out just like he wanted. He went to college, earned his degree in engineering and began his job. He and Justice met up at my wedding. They had both recently ended relationships and took comfort in seeing each other again. The result of that was their son, James, who is now thirteen. They named him after Justice's father, who died while she was pregnant.

They tried to make a relationship work but decided they would be better parents if they were not together. Jon moved to Bettencourt to be close to James about a year later when he could no longer stand the constant traveling to visit his son. The acts of Jon moving and Justice putting their son first restored their faith in each other. They put their differences aside and fell in love. That was more than twelve years ago, and they are still together. They also have a daughter, Cadence, who is a year older than Annie.

Justice recently revealed a secret to me. On the night I almost fell from the lighthouse, she and Jon had a brief make-out session before they gathered the firewood. Bo and I had unknowingly stopped them when they heard us come upstairs for my medicine. They never said anything because they had figured there was no chance of a lasting relationship between the two of them. They were wrong.

Brad joined the Navy after high school just as he planned. The events of September 11, 2001, greatly impacted his career. He will retire soon from the Navy and plans to move back to Arkansas. Brad and his high school girlfriend, Kate, went their separate ways after their graduation. When they met up again a couple of years ago, Kate was divorced and had a young daughter she was raising alone. Brad had gone through a string of broken relationships and had never married. He and Kate are married now and seem to be happy. Brad is a caring stepfather to Kate's daughter.

Jack joined the Army after high school and served back-to-back tours overseas after the events of September 11. We worried about him and prayed for him constantly while he was deployed. After an injury that resulted in the loss of his leg below the knee, he was discharged and went to college to teach science like my father. Jack and his wife have a son and two daughters. They live in Dardanelle.

Trini lives near them with her husband. They are both real estate agents and are expecting a baby early next year. She and I still have a very close relationship. I am thrilled for her and know she will be a wonderful mother.

Dad and Margo are still happily married living in Dardanelle enjoying their grandchildren. They visit us in Bettencourt often. We travel to see them about twice a year now that my children are older.

Bo took over his father's company just as he planned. I teach history at the high school and run the B&B during the summer and holiday breaks. My children and the teenagers I teach have such different lives than I had. Sometimes I miss those simpler days before all the technology and social media.

Several years ago we had new gravestones put on Caroline, Thomas, and Virginia's resting places. The *Bettencourt Ledger* ran a full article reporting that the deaths of Caroline Marshall and Thomas Cooper were likely accidents due to the broken railing discovered during renovations. I allowed them to publish excerpts from her diary. The paper had to be reprinted several times to meet the demand for a copy of the scandalous account of Caroline Marshall's illegitimate child. I figured the statute of limitations had run out on the embarrassment it would have caused her family.

We haven't had any more spirit encounters at the estate, and I haven't gone back to the top of the lighthouse. I never will. The scar on my arm reminds me of that night and sometimes I still have nightmares about falling, but Bo always comforts me. I wake up every day thankful for what my ancestors built and maintained. And then I look at my own family and feel that I am truly blessed.

Twenty years have passed since I first saw Bettencourt Estate and while it has lost its mysteriousness, it has lost none of its beauty.

ABOUT THE AUTHOR:

Brandi Easterling Collins grew up in Arkansas where she still resides with her husband, two children, and two dogs. When she's not writing or reading, she enjoys spending time with her family, thrift store shopping, painting, drawing, and leisurely walks outside.

Caroline's Lighthouse is her first novel. Her other novels include *Jordan's Sister*, *What I Learned That Summer*, and *One Shot*.

For more information, about future publications, visit caniscareyou.com.